She felt li[ke]
a trapped [animal]

Darcy had to do something fast. Thinking she heard him at the door, she clambered onto the windowsill.

Whether or not she would have landed safely on the balcony below, she never found out. For when her feet did leave the windowsill, it wasn't the way she had planned.

Iron-hard hands hauled her back inside. All Darcy was aware of was that Neve had hold of her and one of his hands was clamped firmly around her waist.

She didn't realize his only intention was to get her back inside. All she knew was that she hadn't escaped him, and his other hand had snaked its way onto her breast. It was then that Darcy began to fight.

Distrust
Her Shadow

Jessica Steele

Harlequin Books

TORONTO • NEW YORK • LOS ANGELES • LONDON
AMSTERDAM • PARIS • SYDNEY • HAMBURG
STOCKHOLM • ATHENS • TOKYO • MILAN

Original hardcover edition published in 1982
by Mills & Boon Limited

ISBN 0-373-02555-6

Harlequin Romance first edition June 1983

CHAPTER ONE

MISS Agnes Mary Emsworth, affectionately known by Darcy as just Emmy, was no relation. But as far as Darcy was concerned, she was family. All the family she had.

They were seated at breakfast that Friday in March, lingering longer than was usual when Darcy had a job to go to.

'Aren't you going to work today dear?' asked the elderly lady, who only a couple of months previously Darcy had been fearful was not going to make it into her eighty-second year. Darcy looked fondly across the table at the sweet soul who had once been her mother's nanny, and observed that Emmy now looked to be more her old self now that wretched bronchitis had finally cleared. But she saw no point in reminding her of what she had told her yesterday and the day before; all this week, in fact—that her friend Jane Davis who ran Adaptable Temps, did not have a job for her before Monday.

'Not today,' she said gently. 'Anything special you'd like to do?'

'I have my club this afternoon.'

It was Darcy's turn to be reminded. Proving, she thought happily, that Emmy wasn't as vague as she had thought she was getting to become. It was a week since she had last met up with her small group of ex-nannies and ex-nursing staff, and had remembered it was again Friday.

'I forgot,' Darcy confessed, instantly changing her mind about taking her on some small economical outing somewhere. Emmy would need to rest this morning if she was going out this afternoon—though it wouldn't do to tell her so.

Emmy, for all her advanced years, was still independently minded. And it was no hardship for her to pretend that Emmy looked after her and not the other way around.

'I think I'd better get down to doing some French study this morning,' she said, her face innocent of wiles as she added, 'You wouldn't care to stay in this morning and help me, would you?'

'Of course, dear,' the old lady smiled. 'But first we'll want this table cleared.'

'Will you be working tomorrow, do you think?' asked Emmy, drying dishes at the sink as Darcy washed them.

It was not unusual for Darcy to work Saturday; or Sunday either if a job came up. Money was tight and, Emmy's health permitting, she had told Jane she was available for anything that came in. The trouble was, the agency wasn't yet on its feet and Saturday and Sunday jobs, or even Monday to Friday work, wasn't plentiful.

'I haven't a job before Monday,' she replied, as both of them left the kitchen and Darcy went over to where she kept her text books, French being the order of the morning.

There had always been something to study, she thought, stealing a glance at Emmy half an hour later, a smile curving her warm mouth to see her mother's old nanny had already dozed off in her comfortable chair nearby.

She laid down her pen, wondering not for the first time why she was trying so hard with her studies. Her French didn't seem to be improving, for all she tried so hard. Would the agency ever be called on to supply a bi-lingual secretary anyway? The way things were going it seemed unlikely.

Determined not to be defeatist, Darcy quickly picked up her pen. To date she had studied book-keeping, reception, and telephone duties. Secretarial training had come easiest to her—and then probably because she hadn't had any anxieties at that time.

The page in front of her remained blank as her mind went back to the time when, her schooling finished, her father had objected to her stated intention to go to secretarial school.

'There's no need,' he had said. 'No need at all for you to cram your head full of that stuff. You'll never have to work while I'm alive.'

She hadn't either, she remembered. Not until four years ago had she set foot inside an office that wasn't her father's.

Pain touched her beautiful green-brown eyes as she recalled the news that had reached her and Emmy that her parents had been killed in a train crash while holidaying abroad. She and Emmy had clung together then.

Emmy had always lived with them, her father raising no objection when his lovely young bride, cut off by her parents for daring to marry a furniture-maker, had wanted Emmy with her.

The news of her parents' death was the worst possible. But more bad news had followed. Had her father lived, Darcy was certain he would have found some way out of his difficulties. He would never have gone away on holiday without some plan for saving his cabinet-making firm from going under. But with his death, the desperate straits the firm was in had come to light. And at the end of it all, even their lovely home had had to be sold to cover debts.

Emmy had been more spritely then, and had been in full agreement when Darcy had suggested they come to London where jobs were more plentiful and paid better. Neither of them had given thought that they might go their separate ways.

They had come to London, found a ground floor flat, and the first years had gone comparatively well. Then Emmy had started ailing.

At first her employers had been understanding about her taking time off to look after her. But when time and again she'd had to take more than the odd day off, weeks sometimes, they had in the end been obliged to part with her services. Several times, Darcy recalled, that same polite phrase had been used when her employment had been terminated for non-attendance.

Not that Emmy knew anything about it. As far as she was aware, she had just got fed up with the job she was doing. Emmy's peace of mind was important to her. The dear love had a dread of hospitals; an even bigger dread of being shut away in an old people's home. And never, thought Darcy fiercely, would she have to be shut away, not if she had any say in the matter. Though that didn't stop her from worrying about how much longer they could go on with her losing every new job within the first six months of starting it.

That was why she had been so glad to have bumped into her old school friend Jane Davis—Jane Dexter she had been before her unfortunate marriage. Jane was the same age as her. But whereas at twenty-two Darcy had not seemed to have done anything, Jane had a marriage and divorce behind her, the only good thing to come from her marriage her pride and joy in the shape of three-year-old Edward, her son.

Over a cup of coffee Jane had told her, having had her fill of love, so-called, she was set on being a business woman, and with her small capital had started a temps agency. And then recalling that Darcy had left their country town with Emmy after doing her secretarial training, she had asked after Emmy, and enquired what work Darcy was now doing.

'I'm out of work at the moment,' Darcy had confessed, and had straight away heard Jane offer to take her on the books.

Feeling slightly uncomfortable, she had felt honour bound then to reveal the reason for her dismissal from her last job—only to be delighted to have Jane confide that in the beginning stages of getting the agency going, it would suit her very well if she came to her and could go the occasional week with her having nothing for her. Jane was equally delighted to have her jump at the offer.

From then on Darcy had spent what time she could in swotting to make herself more efficient and up to any job that came her way, the work she did for the agency not being limited to secretarial work.

And so far, she thought, looking down at her still blank page, apart from the financial strain, working for Jane as a temp had been the answer to everything. January had been slack at Adaptable Temps, which left her not feeling guilty that she'd had to take four weeks off to look after Emmy.

As she was on the point of wondering if there would be any work for her after her clerk-typist stint next week, the telephone shrilled. Emmy awoke with a start, but Darcy was already on her feet.

'I'll get it,' she smiled, thinking to make Emmy a nice cup of coffee when she'd dealt with the call. But already the ex-nanny was out of her chair and heading for the kitchen, she saw. How they read each other's minds! she thought, then gave her attention to the phone call, discovering it was Jane with a job for her that day.

'It's only just come in, but it appears to be urgent. Probably missed the post or something,' Jane told her. 'Can you deliver a package to Banbury for me?'

Darcy's mind went quickly to Emmy, calculated that since she'd been well now for a few weeks, given the odd day when she was chesty, and since she would be out at her club that afternoon anyway, she needn't worry about her.

'I could get Myra to do it, if Miss Emsworth is under the weather,' Jane followed on.

'No, it's O.K. I can do it,' Darcy said promptly. They could do with the money.

'Fine. See you in about half an hour, then?'

Darcy went into the kitchen and carried the tray of

coffee Emmy had made back into the sitting room. She didn't really have time for coffee if Jane was expecting her in thirty minutes, but since it was just a driving job she thought her jeans and shirt with her car coat over the top would be all right, no need to change into something smarter. Besides which, if Emmy wasn't to be muddled she would have to explain slowly.

'That was Jane on the phone,' she said when they were both sitting.

'How is her dear little baby?' Emmy asked, never having lost her love of children. 'It's ages since she brought him to see us.'

'He's three now,' Darcy told her, recalling that it was only two weeks since Jane and Edward had popped in. 'I have to go out, Emmy. But I should be home by the time you get back from your club.'

'I'll have a nice dinner ready for you,' and beaming, 'I've never seen such blue eyes on a child. And that black hair too, although it's as straight as pump water. Yours always was wavy. Such beautiful hair, Darcy,' she said, her eyes going to Darcy's wavy tresses.

Darcy's hair was black too. But she headed Emmy away from her reminiscences, taking her coffee in a gulp and earning herself a reproving look.

'I shall have to go,' she said gently. 'Is Mrs Bricknell coming for you?'

'At two o'clock. Will you be back for lunch?'

'No, love. Will you make yourself something from the chicken we had yesterday?'

Emmy came to see her to the door as she always did. 'See you later,' Darcy called, and walked sedately until she was sure the front door had closed, then raced to her car, reaching the office three minutes after the half hour.

'Didn't have time to change—jeans all right?'

'You look just right as you always do,' commented the blonde-haired Jane, picking up a slim package from off her desk. 'I've written it down, but basically all you have to do is deliver this envelope to a Mr Littlejohn in a hotel in Banbury. He's waiting for it, apparently.'

Darcy took the envelope. 'Must be important if they're prepared to pay an agency fee to get it delivered quickly. Any idea what's inside?'

'Not thick enough to contain drugs, if you think you're on a drugs run,' quipped Jane. 'I expect it's some confidential document wanted for a conference this afternoon. I wonder if they'll think of us to fill the gap if some secretary's head is on the chopping block for the oversight,' she mused, her business head taking over before she returned to the matter in hand. 'A Mr Townsend brought it in. He gave a good address and has paid in advance, so all we've got to do is get that package delivered as soon as possible.'

'I can take a hint,' Darcy grinned. 'I'm still clerk-typist on Monday?'

'Sorry,' said Jane, looking worried. 'I know it's under-using your skills, but things are flatter than flat just now.'

'Not to worry, better things are round the corner, I feel sure,' said Darcy, attempting to take the worried look from her face.

'I hope so.'

Given her car, a necessary luxury, was past its first flush of youth, she made it to Banbury in record time. It took her a few extra minutes to find the hotel she had been instructed to go to. But having found it, she parked her car, took up her bag and went inside.

She answered the receptionist's pleasant greeting, then said, 'I'd like to see Mr Littlejohn, please,' and discovered she was expected as the receptionist gave her the room number and turned away to answer the phone.

The job was new to her, and Darcy would have preferred that Mr Littlejohn came down to her, but perhaps the conference had already started.

By dint of the lift and a couple of false turnings

along the corridor, she eventually found the door she was looking for. She tapped smartly, then pinned an efficient smile on her face ready to get in a plug for the agency.

The door was opened by a tall, thickset man, who to her mind looked more like a prizefighter than some executive. He didn't look like the tea boy either, she thought lightly, if he was the one who had been told by the powers that be to see who was at the door.

'Mr Littlejohn?' she said, her smile staying in place, her smile still staying when she saw the look of surprise that took the man. Then he was frowning, and it was her turn to be surprised. For she got only as far as, 'I've called with the delivery you're expecting ...' her 'by courtesy of Adaptable Temps' never uttered, when the man had taken her by the arm, and with one flex of his powerful muscles had yanked her off her feet, and she was inside the room, the door slammed shut.

Abruptly her smile vanished. Open-mouthed, she stared at the man hovering menacingly over her. Fear dried her mouth. She had hit the bed, was half perched on it, and was swallowing hard. There was no time to wonder what was wrong. Time only to know that something was wrong, that something was very, very wrong.

She tried to get on top of her fear as she struggled to her feet. 'What ...' she began chokily, and started to back away as, her eyes going wide, she saw the bathroom door open and another powerfully built man appear, the man looking at her incredulously before the words escaped him:

'He never said it would be a girl!' Then he was coming forward.

'I'm—I'm here to s-see Mr Littlejohn,' Darcy said bravely, in shock still, her eyes looking feverishly around for a way of getting past both men and out through the door she had come in by.

'Where's the letter?' demanded the one who had

opened the door to her, making short work of the small space she had managed to put between them.

And, numbed, Darcy didn't know if it was the realisation that the package she had in her possession must be highly prized, making it essential that she gave it to Mr Littlejohn only, and none other, that she made no attempt to hand it over; or if it was because suddenly as both men loomed over her, she was too petrified, her courage deserting her, for her dry throat to manage even the smallest syllable.

Again she made some attempt to put some space between them, finding she did have some small courage left as, backing to the window she asked, wishing her voice sounded more demanding rather than the squeak that came through:

'What—is all this?'

'She wants to play it the hard way, George,' said one of them, making her think distractedly that he had seen one too many gangster movies by the way he began banging one great fist into the palm of his other hand.

But it was then, realisation hitting her that neither of these two men were play-acting, that they were deadly serious, that a fear greater than any she had ever known took charge of her. Terror gripped the pit of her stomach as they advanced. Then she was past thinking and was feeling only as her eyes going huge she saw the two men loom closer.

And as one great hairy hand looked to be coming out to take her by the throat, the alarm in her that had her staring transfixed, unbelieving, reached a crescendo. And as a roaring sounded in her ears, so a grey mist of terrified comprehension of her fate, swirled up and around her, and Darcy knew neither fear nor terror then as, mercifully, she fainted.

The blackness of her faint began to form patterns of grey again. Through shadowed mists she strove to open her eyes. Vaguely she was aware of three men in the room, but she knew no panic then, her mind too be-

fuddled for her to know where she was or how many
men there had been in the room before.

Someone gave her something to drink, then told her
to swallow something. She obliged simply because she
didn't have enough thinking power to wonder why she
shouldn't, and heard that same voice, drifting now in
her ears, say, 'She'll be all right.'

Darcy didn't have a worry in the world, as she heard
that calm voice go on to say something about her sleeping. She closed her eyes; to sleep sounded a good idea.

There was a pain in her head. Darcy groaned softly and
opened her eyes. Then for a moment, conscious only of
pain, nothing else registered. She closed her eyes, then
opened them again. She had no idea where she was, but
something in her subconscious seemed to be telling her
that she wasn't in bed, that she wasn't at home with
Emmy.

Yet the room was in darkness, the way her room at
the flat would be if it was night and she had just
awakened. And she was lying on something too—and
yet her bed was softer than this, wasn't it?

Perhaps she'd been dreaming, a bad dream. That
would account for the flutter of panic she felt in her
insides. She stretched out a hand to reach for her table
lamp, and discovered she didn't appear to have enough
strength to keep her arm aloft. Yet she made her arm
stay outstretched, because several things struck her just
then. She had a fairly sizeable bruise on her arm she
had no memory of. And since she could see that bruise,
then the room couldn't be in complete darkness as she
had at first thought.

Her arm fell, she hadn't the strength to sustain it.
That worried her for a second until the feel of cold
leather on her arm stirred her to investigate what it was
she had been sleeping on.

It was a leather couch. She didn't have a leather
couch! No one she knew had a black leather couch. To
be able to see it was black leather brought her woolly

mind back to realise there had to be a light on in the room somewhere.

Darcy turned her head. Light hit her eyes, forcing her to close them as excruciating pain was added to the throbbing in her temples. She waited another few seconds for the pain to ease, then slowly lifted her eyelids.

This time she was able to make out there was a desk in the room, a huge desk. On the desk reposed a lamp, a purely functional affair, and that, she saw, was where the light was coming from.

Suddenly Darcy was catching her breath. There was a dark shape behind that desk! Someone had been there while she slept! Did she know that someone? Her head felt too full of pain for her to cope with the question. But whoever it was, he obviously didn't see any great need to disturb himself too much, for his masculine hand was calmly working away on the paper in front of him, not allowing anything to distract him from it.

Urgently Darcy tried to find her tongue. Then she discovered, along with her throbbing head, that her throat was parched dry, nothing but a thick croak leaving her.

But in the silence of the room the man behind the desk must have heard it, she thought. Must too, she thought hazily, have seen her arm waving about in the air. And yet he was making not the least sign that he was aware of her, whatever he was doing being apparently of far more importance than any need she might have.

About to try for his attention once more, Darcy just then had ample proof that he was well aware of her existence. For, without taking his eyes from what he was doing, that gold pen in his hand still moving over the paper beneath it—that in itself telling her he had little concern for her—he spoke.

'So, Miss Alexander,' he said, his voice uncompromising, 'finally you've come round.'

The voice that had come from that dark shape was well educated, but that did nothing to ease the flutter of panic in her that was growing rather than diminishing that at last she had made contact with another human being.

'Wh-who are you?' she croaked from her dry throat. And with memories trying to get in of other voices, of voices that hadn't held his cultured accents, panic was in her voice as she quickly asked, 'Where am I?'

Some memory came back then. Hurried in, fear racing in with it. She remembered with terrifying clarity that hotel room somewhere, and was trying to swallow her fear as she saw the man lay his gold pen down on the desk.

She saw him move, and for a moment as he got to his feet, she forgot that his voice was different. For he seemed, from where she was lying, to be higher than a house, and in that brief instant she thought it was the same thug who had hauled her into that hotel room.

But even while she was wondering was she still in that same hotel, the man moved round his desk, came nearer, and she could see that tall though he was, he didn't have the bulk of that other man.

Her head was muzzy, and sleep wanted to claim her as the tall man stood in front of her blocking out that painful light. But she must now allow herself to drift off back to sleep again. She had no idea how long she had been asleep, as it was, no idea what time it was—and not an earthly idea of what was going on.

Pain hit her again as the man took a seat that had been next to the couch, only she hadn't seen it; the room appeared lighter now she was getting used to it, the man no longer blocked the light.

'Who are you?' she asked again, in fear that he, like that other man, might be going to take hold of her.

Her eyes sped in search of his hands, her fear abating as her eyes noted the broken skin on one of his knuckles, but her mind was unable to stay with one thought for very long just then, lighting down on the notion that from his hand it looked as though he had recently been in a fight. Her thoughts then jumped on as she tried to equate that wound with those long sensitive fingers.

Then any fleeting idea that he might be sensitive was sent on its way when in reply to her question he answered, aggression only there:

'You're saying you don't know who I am?'

It sank in that he sounded as though he thought she knew him from somewhere. He sounded positive in fact, she thought. And for the first time she looked at him, could see his features clearly now that he was sitting. But the more she looked at him, the more positive she was that she had never before met him.

He looked to be somewhere past his middle thirties, she thought, as she stared at his grim features. Her eyes went down to his severe mouth, a mouth that appeared never to have learned how to smile; and on to a chin that was square and firm, a chin that said he didn't suffer fools gladly. She raised her eyes past his sharp nose and met his eyes, eyes that had her doubly convinced she had never before met him. She had worked for various employers, even prior to her joining the agency, but he was not one of them. No one she knew had eyes dark as the night that pierced straight through you and looked to be able to see into your very soul, she was certain of that.

'I've—never met y-you,' she said, wishing her voice was stronger, wishing she felt stronger. But she didn't feel strong. She felt as weak as a kitten.

He had no comment to make about her declaration that she had never met him. He just sat there studying her—studying her face which she was sure, if it was anything like she felt, must be several shades paler than its normal faintly tinted olive.

At that moment she felt too exhausted to do anything but let him look at her until he got tired of doing so and eventually told her what all this was about. But when he continued to sit, seeming in no hurry to tell her anything, a spark of anger forced its way through her feeling of lethargy.

Silent anger in her reached a peak. It had her wanting

to demand who did he think he was that he could send
his henchmen—for he had to be boss, it was written all
over him—around the country terrifying innocent
females.

But she was wary of him too. She remembered, now
that the fog in her brain was thinning, of the pugnacious
way those two men had looked ready to attack her. The
state her strength was in just then, she knew this man
would need no other help if he was like-minded.

'H-how do you know my name?' she enquired, certain
she hadn't been asked it, much less volunteered it.

'Your driving licence was in your bag,' she was coolly
told, no shame anywhere about him that he had calmly
rooted through her belongings.

Darcy swallowed that, as she tried to think what other
information her driving licence gave. She recalled that
the age of the holder could be worked out from it, then
said goodbye to anger as it raced away and fear rushed
in and grabbed her by the throat—fear for Emmy. Her
address was on her driving licence! Her address and
Emmy's. This man, those other men, they must all be
crooks. Oh, let them leave Emmy alone, she prayed. She had
no idea what they were after, but . . . The question couldn't be
contained.

'You haven't been—to my home?'

'At the moment I see little point. I have you here,'
said her captor coldly. And obscurely, 'If anyone wants
you I'm sure they'll know exactly where to look.' And
while she was chewing on that, he dropped his cool
manner and the aggression she had heard before was
showing again when he said grimly, 'The address in your
driving licence—is that where you live with Stoddart?'

The name Stoddart meant nothing to her, nor the fact
that this man thought she might be living with him.
More important was that the thugs this man employed,
or the man himself, went nowhere near Emmy.

'I live alone,' she said quickly. 'Quite alone.'

The grunt she received as answer told her nothing,
causing her to wish she hadn't asked the question had

he been to her home. She didn't want him thinking about her home, that she might have something to hide there. She would have done far better, she thought, not to have referred to her home at all. Though it wasn't surprising, with her head aching the way it was, that her thinking was less than sharp. She tried to get him away from the subject of where she lived, a spurt of anger rearing as she challenged:

'It's against the law to . . .'

'Against the law!' Harshly she was cut off. 'What do you think blackmail is—some sweet juvenile pastime?'

'*Blackmail!*' Scepticism wasn't the word for the cynical disbelief that was in his expression at her startled exclamation. 'You're in this up to your dainty neck,' the man growled. 'Don't try coming the innocent with me, Miss Alexander. I've been wise to women from a very early age.' She didn't doubt it, he looked to have slept with more than a honing stone for company, but she didn't think to say so, she wanted to go home, home to Emmy. 'You're in this for all you can get out of it,' he went on to snarl. 'Only this time,' he threatened darkly, 'you've tangled with someone who's going to see you get all you deserve—and more!'

Rampant fear was with her. She wasn't sure, apart from when she had been blissfully asleep, that it had ever left. He had that look on him that said he meant every word. And she didn't know then, waves of sleep still hovering, how she was going to get through to him that she had done nothing wrong.

'Look, Mr . . .' He looked, but did not offer his name. Darcy licked dry lips. 'Look,' she said hoarsely, 'I haven't a clue what's going on. I've never bl-blackmailed anyone in my life,' she continued, despite his look that said he didn't believe a word. Fleetingly she wondered what anyone could have on him that he should be open to blackmail. But the thought didn't stay as she strove, urgently now, to try and get him to see that she was totally innocent of the charge. 'I think blackmail is a disgusting trade,' she said earnestly.

Her green-brown eyes fixed on his, she waited to see if she had got through to him. But his expression changed not one iota as she came to the end.

'You don't believe me, do you?' she said flatly.

'Lady, you'll be telling me the truth before we're through,' he said shortly, sending sharp darts of alarm shooting through her. 'You can make up your mind to that.'

'But there's nothing to tell you!' Darcy cried, her head thundering so badly she was having a hard time in trying to recall just why it was she had gone to that hotel at all. Fresh spears of pain assaulted her, causing her to close her eyes, and her shaky hand went to her temple. 'Oh, my head!' she groaned, and heard him move. Her eyes flew open, and she flinched back as she saw he was standing, that he was bending over her. Fear panicked her, had her blurting out her fear. 'Don't—d-don't...' Her voice faded into nothing at the grim tight-lipped look of him.

'Stay just where you are,' he gritted. 'I'll get you something for your head.'

Surprise had her doing just that. She stayed where she was for all of thirty seconds, some instinct coming to tell her that she was not still in that hotel after all, but in a private house.

Her brow wrinkled as that knowledge came. She would have thought he would have sent his servants to do his bidding. Yet surprise number one had been that he had recognised her need for aspirin as a real one. And surprise number two—that he had gone for the aspirin himself.

Then all thought fled on the memory of his last remark. 'Stay just where you are,' he had said. Fool that she was, she had wasted precious seconds in lying there when she should be setting about making her escape.

The idea upon her she saw he had left the door open. In a flash she had swung her legs off the couch. The next second she was on her feet ready to run. And the next second, she was stupefied to find, as she went crashing to the floor, that her legs just wouldn't hold her!

CHAPTER TWO

TRYING to keep a lid on panic that she didn't have the strength of a gnat, Darcy was still sitting helplessly when the man who had gone for something for her headache came striding back into the room.

He saw at once the result of her pathetic attempt at flight and threw her a grim look that boded nothing good for her as he placed the glass of water he was carrying down upon the desk and came to stand over her.

But that look he had tossed her way, that look that said she was in for some rough treatment, was sufficient to have her using every ounce of energy she could muster to try and make it away from him.

She did not make it a foot from him. Hard hands, long arms, were reaching down for her, had lifted her without effort, and Darcy was swallowing hard. The words to tell him to leave her alone were locked in her throat at the almost tangible distaste she sensed was coming from her captor that he was having to soil his hands and touch her.

Wordlessly, held aloft in his arms, she found herself staring into those piercing black eyes. His glance fastened on her, then his jaw tightened. And it was without ceremony, entirely unmoved by the scared look of her, that he dumped her back to where she had tried her bid for freedom.

He reached behind him for the glass, his voice more of a growl, as he said, 'I told you to stay put.'

But Darcy's panic was spilling over, had her ignoring that he did not sound very pleased with her. 'Why can't I walk?' she asked agitatedly. 'What have you done to me?'

The glass in his hand, he was insensitive to her look

of panic, his expression that of a cynic as he said, 'I've done nothing to you—yet,' that threat again not making her feel any better. 'I should have realised Stoddart's accomplice would be female,' he went on, and the name Stoddart again registered with Darcy, before he unbent a fraction to inform her, 'You banged your head when you fainted. You're still under the effects of the medication a visiting doctor to the hotel administered.'

Her panic subsided a little as her powers of rationalisation went to work. She had no memory of fainting, but, as other patches of memory cleared, she didn't wonder that she had. She must have banged her head pretty solidly too to have frightened those thugs into calling for a doctor, she realised—and realised too, though not liking them any the more, that those two men had not been about to murder her as had looked likely, since they must have immediately sought medical assistance.

Her strength would return, she saw. She would be able to walk again just as soon as the effects of whatever strong dose of medication she had been given had worn off. With that rationalisation, she began to feel better. Better, and angry at all that had befallen her.

'I wonder why they bothered calling in a doctor,' she said disagreeably. 'I wouldn't have thought thugs like that would have . . .'

'Thugs?' He seemed surprised that that was how she had seen them. 'Hardly thugs,' he said, and told her, although she didn't believe a word of it, 'They were merely a couple of the most trustworthy security men I happen to know.'

A likely tale, she thought sourly. 'Huh,' she scoffed. 'Do security men often go around looking ready to flatten innocent females?'

She saw her reference to her innocence had done nothing to sweeten him. 'But they didn't flatten you, did they?' he said toughly. 'They were under specific instructions not to dish out any rough stuff.' And with barely a pause, he added, 'I personally wanted to serve myself what had been earned.'

Her anger fled at the implication behind his words. Fear was there again as she gasped, 'Y-you mean you—you intend to beat me up?'

He threw her a look of disdain, then slowly, he owned, 'That had been my intention.'

'It—er—it isn't any longer?' Her throat felt drier than ever.

'Do you want this cure for your headache or not?'

His sharp words had her eyes going to the tablets he had in his hand, her question left unanswered. The tablets were tinfoil-wrapped, a well known painkiller. She took them from him, glad of the glass of water, and was so thirsty that after downing the tablets, she drank all of it. And only then did she feel anywhere near to trying to cope with the situation she found herself in. Though her voice was still husky as she made herself ask:

'What—are you going to do with me?'

Not returning to the chair he had been seated in earlier, he stood leaning against the desk, light from the lamp coming from the right of him. Then, with Darcy afraid to look away from him, he stayed that way, looking down at her through narrowed eyes, not saying a word, but for an age immobile as he contemplated her on the black leather couch. Her nerves stretched, shot, she was on the verge of starting to scream out her innocence, and then he spoke, his voice almost casual, as he threw the question back at her.

'What would you suggest I do with a blackmailer's accomplice?'

'I'm not . . .' she began rapidly, then stopped as he moved, irritated with her. She knew then that he wasn't going to believe her if she stayed there forever denying she had any part in it. She took a long breath trying to steady herself. 'Stoddart is the blackmailer, of course,' she said. There was a blank somewhere in her mind, it would clear when the effects of that medication wore off, she was sure, but even so, she felt convinced that she didn't know anyone called Stoddart.

'Your memory is starting to improve,' was the sarcastic reply. 'Keep going, you'll have it all soon.'

'Give me a hint,' she dared. And at his look that said he didn't want any lip from the likes of her, 'Well, it's not my fault if I've got a lump of cotton wool for a brain.'

'You're saying your memory has gone?' was the mocking enquiry.

'No,' she said huffily. 'Some things are very clear— such as being in a hotel room somewhere with a couple of thugs who looked ready to murder me.' She had said the word 'thugs' deliberately so he should know she wasn't any nearer to believing that they were the security men he had called them. But involuntarily she shuddered at the memory, then had the strangest idea that some of the hardness went from him as he witnessed her shudder. But his face was hard again as she added, 'But—but for the life of me, I can't remember why I went there.'

'Mr Littlejohn.'

The name was dropped into the air. It added to her confusion. 'I thought you said Stoddart,' she said. Then as memory came to tease. 'Ye-es—Littlejohn,' she said, desperately pushing to remember. 'I was to ask . . .' Light suddenly came through, and with it overwhelming relief. She couldn't believe she was a blackmailer. He had known that she had nothing to do with that filthy trade. And she knew too, now, that she had the means to prove it. 'I was delivering a package,' she said, and her relief was so great, she even managed a weak smile.

The man towering above her saw it, and she saw straight away as the hardness in him set into solid agression, his hands bunching into fists, that he didn't think too much to it.

'If you're smiling because you've just remembered that Stoddart was to pick up twenty thousand pounds this morning, then don't,' he advised her icily, as he rubbed his knuckles as though at some pleasing reminder, regardless that one of his knuckles was skinned. 'I gave him something he wasn't expecting.' And while Darcy was going under at the mention of twenty thousand pounds, not to mention the satisfaction in his grim voice that told her he personally had beaten Stoddart to a pulp, he was adding, 'Something I don't think he'll forget in a hurry.'

'That same something you personally intended to give his accomplice?' she said swallowing. And, not certain, if she couldn't get her words in first that she wouldn't yet be receiving the hiding of her life, almost tripping over her words, she was hurriedly telling him, 'But I'm not Stoddart's accomplice. I don't even know the man. I-I work for Adaptable Temps, it's a London agency, and b-because I d-didn't have any work on today, when a man went in and asked . . .'

'What man?' he interrupted, fully aware of her fear she knew that, his disbelieving interruption doing nothing to alleviate it.

'That's what I'm trying to tell you, if you'll give me a chance. This Mr . . . Mr . . .' Damn, she couldn't remember his name. She saw from the way he was leaning back against the desk again that he thought, still under the tail end of the doctor's medication as she was, that her powers of invention were not fully with her.

'How about Smith?' was the unwanted sarcastic offer.

'It wasn't Smith,' she said irritably. 'It was . . .' It wouldn't come. 'I'll remember in a minute,' she said, sure of it.

'Meantime,' he suggested, 'why not go on with the fairy story?'

Darcy threw him a look of intense dislike. 'It's the truth,' she said snappily—and earned herself a look that said, don't take that tone with me if you don't want your ears boxed. 'It is,' she said stonily. 'Jane Davis who runs the agency rang me this morning and said this man had called in with a package he wanted delivered to a Mr Littlejohn at a hotel in—in Banbury.'

She could have saved her breath, she saw. He still wasn't believing her, that much was as plain as day. Agitatedly she pushed a wing of dark hair back from her face, noticing for the first time, and with shock that stopped all thought for a moment, that she had a tear about eight inches long in the sleeve of her shirt.

'You can prove all this, of course?' His expression was openly discounting all she had said as his eyes followed to where hers had gone, to where her shoulder was peeping out through the tear in her shirt.

Knowing she was just about to make him fall flat on his cynical, disbelieving face, Darcy was able to hold down the discomfort she felt that he was finding her bare shoulder of some interest.

Quickly she told him the agency's telephone number. 'Ring the agency,' she said, suddenly feeling better than she had in a long while. 'Not only will you find the agency actually exists, but Jane Davis will be able to tell you all about the job she sent me on.'

If she had been expecting him to leap to the telephone, then she was in for a disappointment, for he didn't budge an inch. Exhilaration left her. Oh no, she thought, was all that talk of him being blackmailed all so much baloney? Was he a crook, those other men criminals? What the heck was going on?

'Why—why don't you ring?' she asked, her voice gone from being husky to being hoarse.

He smiled—a smile that to her over-activated nerves had something sinister in it. 'This agency stays open all night, does it?'

He had dropped his question out quietly. But Darcy just wasn't with him. She didn't grasp his meaning, and it showed in her mystified look. He consulted his watch, his only concession to helping her out.

'It's ten past four in the morning,' he told her laconically, unknowingly taking her thoughts scooting away from the predicament in which she found herself.

Ten past four in the morning! Emmy! The poor love would be going hairless with worry. Darcy's mind leapt

on; to Emmy calling the police, of the police checking
with Jane, of them going to that hotel in Banbury . . .

Her thoughts broke off. Just in case the police weren't
going to come banging on the door at any moment, she
had to try and convince this big aggressive man in front
of her that she had never ever been involved in any
blackmail plot. She had to get back to Emmy.

'Jane always switches the answering machine on when
she goes home at night,' she said hurriedly. 'If you ring
that number I gave you, it will give you Jane's home
number to ring.' The lift of an eyebrow told her he
remained unconvinced, and Darcy found herself gabbl-
ing on. 'Sometimes if Jane has something on she uses
my number, or that of one of the other girls . . .' Her
voice tailed off—he didn't trust a word of it. 'Only I'm
sure she'll be at home,' she tacked on lamely, 'since she
said nothing about not being there.'

'Why not give me her home number to start with?' he
queried loftily, stinging Darcy to throw him a look of
dislike.

'Because I didn't know what time it was. And anyway,
you wouldn't believe any such agency existed unless you
heard the recording machine answer "Adaptable
Temps",' she said stiffly.

'You could just be right there,' he said, letting her
know he was playing some game with her for his own
enjoyment; that he had already thought that one out.
But still he made no move to pick up the phone on his
desk. 'This agency is available to take on work any time,
day or night, is it?' he asked, his tone baiting.

'We advertise "Any job, Any time, Any place",' she
said woodenly, hating him and his sneering, cynical
tongue.

'Sounds as though the agency is desperate for work.'

His sarcasm had gone. Darcy looked into those piercing black eyes—stared, and thought she saw what might
be a hint of something that said he might, he just might,
be giving credence to what she was saying.

She got ready to work on that hope. It was neither

here nor there to him how the agency was doing, but at least there seemed to be a chance she might be getting through to him. Surely if she told him all she could about the agency he would see she wasn't making it up? If she worked on any doubt in his mind then at the very least he would ring the number she had given him to check. He would know then that she had been speaking nothing but the truth, Jane would soon . . .

'It's a slack time of year,' she began, hanging fast on to hope. 'Business isn't very good at the moment.'

'In fact the agency is struggling?'

It was, but she didn't want to tell him that. 'Er—yes,' she said in a rush, seeing something in him that said any glimmer of hope she had could disappear. She swallowed the feeling of being disloyal to Jane, knowing how important it was that he understood, believed. 'Normally I think Jane would have been more cautious about the job she gave me today, but at the moment, she's glad of any job that comes in.'

Silently he looked at her when she had finished, and she would have given anything to know what was going on behind those dark all-seeing eyes.

'Please ring her,' she pleaded, thoughts of Emmy going out of her mind with worry coming back to plague her. 'Jane will tell you . . .' She stopped. He had moved.

Relief ready to swamp her, she saw him go to the other side of the desk and pick up the phone. She even smiled, knowing her ordeal was nearly over. The effect of the medication was wearing away now too, she thought, as she observed the tall man's fingers as he dialled the number she had given him, that skinned knuckle causing her smile to dip as she recalled he had given instructions that she wasn't to be beaten up, that he was saving that pleasure for himself.

In haste her eyes went from his hands. He had finished dialling. Thank goodness she had escaped whatever retribution he had in mind for her for being 'up to her dainty neck' in some blackmail plot, she thought. Then as her eyes went to his face, she frowned. The answering

machine must have given him Jane's home number by
now, yet he was writing nothing down.

Her frown stayed in place. She had learned a little
about him, she thought. She didn't doubt he would not
take everything she had said as being gospel just because
the recording had answered 'Adaptable Temps', not
without ringing Jane first—not him. Her frown cleared
as the thought came, perhaps he had the sort of mind
that could easily remember telephone numbers. Perhaps
he had no need to write it down.

But something was wrong! His face had never
shown any sort of pleasantness to her, but now it was
looking grimmer than ever. He was still holding on to
the phone, but the relief that had been hers started to
dwindle. For suddenly she was being fixed by a pair
of piercing eyes, and fresh disquiet was coming roaring
in.

'What's—wrong?' Would her voice never lose that
hoarse note of fear?

She watched while he manoeuvred the phone across
the desk, stretching the flex until he had pulled it so it
would reach her. He then held out the instrument so she
could hear for herself the tone ringing out again and
again, with no machine cutting in to answer.

'You've dialled the wrong number,' she said at once.
'The phone is always switched to the recording, always.'
She saw the ominously quiet way in which he placed the
phone back on its rest, and was in there quickly to insist,
'You *must* have dialled wrong,' she knew it for a fact.
'Jane is too concerned about the lack of business to ever
forget . . .'

'Perhaps you'd like to dial the number yourself,' he
suggested, ice that would blunt many a pickaxe before it
would crack there in his voice.

By way of some more manoeuvring, he was calling
her bluff by handing the phone to her where she was
huddled up on the couch, cold sarcasm fairly dripping
as he suggested:

'You have no objection, I hope, if I look over your

shoulder to check that you call only the number you gave me to dial?'

Darcy ignored him. She could afford to, if *his* story was true. *He* must have dialled incorrectly. She wasn't surprised to see her fingers were shaking as she dialled the office number. She was sure it would take her all of a week to get over this little episode. The next time Jane had a delivery job like this one, she could send Myra. Myra was a hard case, able to cope with anything that came her way; wolfish employers, anything, Myra came out on top in any situation.

The first three ringing out tones sounded in Darcy's ears. Then disbelief was showing in her face as they sounded a fourth, and a fifth time. She was certain she had dialled the number right, but instead of hearing 'This is Adaptable Temps, would you please . . .' all she was getting was the continuous ringing out sound.

'I must have dialled it wrong,' she said, and would have gone through the procedure again, only she didn't get the chance. The phone was taken from her and placed with a none too gentle thud on the desk, just as though the man who was threatening her with dire consequences had had enough.

'You did *not* dial it wrong,' he said forcefully, letting her know he had followed every digit. And pausing only briefly, 'So what now, Miss Alexander?'

'What now?'

'Surely your quick, devious little brain has got another stalling plan in mind.'

'I wasn't stalling—I wasn't!' she protested, shattered that there had been no reply. 'I can't understand it. I honestly can't. Jane *always* switches over to the recording whenever she leaves the office. The agency, the chance of another job coming in, is much too important for her to forget.'

'You're getting to sound repetitious,' she was told, which irked her, because she didn't care whether he found her boring or not. He wasn't in the hot seat as she was.

'Let me go,' she pleaded. 'I promise I can straighten

all this out. Jane will phone you tomorrow. I'll—I'll get her to come and see you . . .'

'It's tomorrow already,' he told her flatly.

'Let me go,' she tried again, knowing she was wasting her time. He was hard, she could see that, contemptuous of her pleading. 'Then tell me where I am,' she begged, some vague notion of escape coming to her.

'When you admit you're in this up to your ears,' was the uncompromising reply.

'But there's nothing to adm . . .'

His exasperated breath, the look on his face that said he was fed up with her and her lies, stopped her. She saw disgust in his face too, disgust at the filthy plot he thought she had been party to in order to get some easy money.

'What—what are you going to do with me?' she asked, knowing with dread in her heart that the retribution she thought she had escaped was going to be exacted in full.

It did nothing to help when she saw the way his eyes went over her. Fresh fear stormed in, gripped at her as she saw his eyes light on that part of her bare shoulder that just wouldn't stay covered up. The over-long pause that followed having every nerve tense in her body, his softly spoken words that came at last, doing nothing to release that tension when, eventually, he drawled:

'I think for a start we'll go to bed.'

For all of two seconds Darcy was too shocked to say anything. And then as all hell let loose in her at his softly drawled words, she was cowering back, gasping, 'No!' her hand flying to her shoulder in a vain attempt to cover up her naked flesh. 'Oh no,' she whispered, huddling as far away from him as she could to one end of the couch.

She heard his hard mirthless laugh as he witnessed the way she was backing away from him. It reached her ears as insulting. As though he was saying that hard up, he wasn't. He confirmed what she thought she had heard in his mirthless laughter.

'I wouldn't sully myself by touching you that way, so

drag your not so pure little mind up, Miss Alexander,'
he told her brutally. And with not a laugh about him,
he ordered, 'On your feet!'

Although he had made no bones about not being
physically interested in her, she was much too shaken to
believe him. 'I'll stay here,' she said, making no move to
leave the couch.

'A patient man I am not,' he gritted. And she soon
discovered that when it came to decisions about her
staying on the couch, the option just wasn't hers.

A squeak of alarm left her when those long arms
reached down for her, realisation coming, as with ease
he hoisted her up, that she just hadn't the strength yet
to kick and claw at him.

Her heart hammering frantically against her ribs, she
felt herself being carried from the room. Light blinded
her eyes, making her turn her face into his shoulder as
he flicked a switch to illuminate the way up the stairs.

She stayed quiet as, his breathing remaining even,
untroubled by the weight he was carrying, the tall man
took her up two flights of stairs and to one of the upper
rooms. But no way did she trust him, and she was con-
serving what energy she had for the battle she thought
might still come regardless of what he had said about
not sullying himself by touching her.

He pressed a light switch in the room, and Darcy
tensed in his arms as she wondered if it would have
been better to try and make a bolt for it before he had
brought her up those stairs. Yet he would have grabbed
her before she had made it more than a yard past him,
if she had got that far.

Trembling, she realised he had halted, and regardless
of the light hurting her eyes, she turned her face to stare
into those piercing eyes that were looking down at her.
Eyes that told her here was a man who gave no quarter.

Darcy looked away from him, saw the bed and knew
that her strength even when she was fit would never be
up to his all male strength, yet still she was ready to
fight him tooth and nail when the crunch came. What

else could she do? She had tried all ways to get through
to him, she thought, more afraid than ever. What else
was there?

Out of nowhere all at once came the remembrance
that he must have a streak of humanity in him somewhere, otherwise he would never have stirred himself to
go and get something for her violent headache, would
he? Would it do any good to try to appeal to that streak
of humanity? It would mean telling him . . . She thought
he was about to move nearer the bed again, and there
just wasn't time to ponder the issue, and words came
blurting from her:

'I'm a—a virgin.'

Her stark statement, the stark plea behind her statement for him not to touch her, fell brittlely into the
quiet of the room. But Darcy made herself look up at
him, stared at him without blinking so he should know
the truth of her statement.

He looked back, straight into her green-brown eyes,
her words causing him to pause had it been his intention
to take her to that bed. But he was no nearer now to
believing her than he had ever been, that much was clear.
And then somehow, when she had been certain he was
going to make some comment refuting her statement—
whether he read the exhaustion she was feeling in her
face, she knew not—he had changed whatever he had
been going to say she was sure of it, and grated:

'You'll forgive me, I'm sure, for not wanting to be
the first.'

Abruptly then he set her to her feet, taking firm hold
of her when her legs threatened to cave in. He still held
on to her with one hand while with the other he opened
a door close by.

'There's the bathroom,' he told her shortly. 'I'll wait
here. Don't lock the door.' Having said that, he saw her
safely inside, saw she had the wall for support, and left
her.

Wearily Darcy sat on the edge of the bath. It was
urgent that she started plotting her escape, she knew

that, but oddly she could find no urgency in her. She felt so tired—so tired.

Some five minutes later, having sluiced her face in cold water in an attempt to revive herself, she was drying herself on the fluffiest of towels, when a heavy hand sounded on the door.

'Are you all right in there?'

It was no thanks to him if she wasn't. 'I'm coming,' she said. The towel slipped from her shaking fingers. Automatically she bent to retrieve it. The bathroom door swung open just as the floor came up to meet her.

In an instant strong arms were round her. The room was spinning, everywhere was moving. When the room righted itself she discovered she was lying on the bed—discovered that efficient fingers were removing her shoes, that efficient hands were coming to the waistband of her jeans.

'No!' she said sharply, coming to rapidly as he favoured her with a grim look.

'Suit yourself.' He straightened up. He seemed about to leave, then hesitated. 'Can you manage by yourself?'

'Perfectly,' she said as snappily as the remnants of the dizziness in her would allow. But still he seemed to hesitate.

'Are you—hungry?' came from him as if against his will. 'Do you want something to eat?'

Was it possible he was concerned she might have gone dizzy through lack of food? 'I want you to go,' she retorted. 'I want to sleep.' She turned her head where she could no longer see him, hoping that he would take the hint that the sooner he left her alone, the better she would like it.

Silence stretched. Make him go, she prayed. Oh, please make him go! She heard a movement, heard the sound of a door handle being turned, and hope leapt in her tired body. The door opened, and closed, and tears started to her eyes. Then she heard a key being inserted, heard the key turn.

So she was his prisoner! Her jailer, that tall, aggressive

man. A man who was cynical about women. A man who, instinct told her, had no illusions about women. A hard and remorseless man. And yet—a man who *did* have some humanity in his soul. Against his judgment, or so it had seemed, he had sufficient humanity in his soul to ask a woman he thought was a partner to blackmailing him if she was hungry.

She sighed, and wiped away tears with the back of her hand. Lord, she was tired!

Daylight had arrived when Darcy awakened. She opened her eyes and stared round at the large, high-ceilinged bedroom. She saw its well kept highly polished antique furniture, and memory stirred.

Then memory was stampeding in, and in moments she had recollection of every nightmarish thing that had happened. Full memory was there of that cold ruthless man who last night, or rather early this morning, had carried her to this very room. She had a memory too of the wretched pathetic creature she had been.

Mortified that she hadn't started to slam into him the moment she had come round from sleep, Darcy realised that the dosage the doctor had administered must be to blame, that she hadn't gone for him the moment she had been aware of him in that room downstairs.

It had to be that, she reasoned. For surely she had more spirit than to calmly submit to some man so easily carrying her upstairs? Why, he could have done anything with her!

She shuddered at the thought of what might have happened to her, and further memory returned. Had she really told him she was a virgin? Not that he had believed her, his intent had not been that way inclined anyway, so she could have kept that little snippet of information to herself.

But she was appalled to find that with the terrible position she was in, she had *actually* fallen asleep the minute the key had turned in that lock. She felt better on recalling that on top of what must have been a massive sedative of some kind, she had downed a couple of painkillers—no wonder she had been so weak knee'd. Well, he needn't think she was going to be so lily-livered today. Just wait until she saw him.

A padded quilt was over her, something she had no recollection of covering herself with. She pushed it aside placing her bare feet on the floor and observing that she was still wearing her jeans and her torn shirt. She filed those facts away, more interested in seeing if her feet would hold her.

With the thick cream carpet beneath her, she discovered, the re-awakening spirit in her surging, that she had perfect balance. She let out a tightly held breath to know that this morning she was one hundred per cent Darcy Alexander, no remains of medication to make her the wilting figure of womanhood she had been.

The light of warfare entered her eyes, then was weakened briefly by thoughts of poor dear Emmy coming to her. Poor Emmy, who last night would have had to look after herself. Not wanting her fighting spirit to be weakened, Darcy tried to avoid thinking about Emmy and the state she must be in that she hadn't come home all night.

She wanted to be as tough as that brute when she saw him again. She couldn't afford to show any signs that she wasn't, she thought, as she went into the bathroom.

Seconds later she was in the bedroom again. She didn't trust her jailer an inch, and went back into the bathroom carrying a straight-backed chair, which, as a further precaution after she had locked the door, she wedged under the handle. She then stripped off and had a quick bath, looked with distaste at the only clothes she had with her, and knew there was nothing else for it, she would have to put them back on again.

Investigating a cabinet in the bathroom, she saw a cellophane-wrapped toothbrush, the seal unbroken. She saw no earthly reason why she should not avail herself of it, or the toothpaste either. That there wasn't a brush or a comb in sight was her misfortune, she thought, as she pushed her sleep tumbled locks back behind her ears.

She unlocked the door and headed out, carrying the chair in front of her.

'Going in for lion-taming?'

Her eyes shot to the man calmly seated in one of the two powder blue chairs in the room. She saw his eyes on her tousled hair and knew she looked a wreck.

'Does this establishment have such a thing as a comb?' she asked hostilely, his hard voice known immediately, only now was she getting him as a person into perspective. It sapped some of her spirit to see him there so unexpectedly, to see he was all virile male, broad-shouldered and with aggressive features, the firmness of his jaw reminding her that he was determined some way or other to have his pound of flesh.

She saw his eyes glint at her tone, but her spirit given a nudge that he was the first man ever to believe she was a liar—leaving aside that he thought she was a blackmailer—and she was again ready for battle.

'You have a comb in your bag,' he reminded her shortly. And it did not help matters to be reminded also that he had rooted among her private things.

'I'm aware of that, but since I haven't seen my bag since yest...' She broke off as his eyes indicated her bag on the floor beside the bed. 'If you've called just to deliver something that's mine anyway,' she resumed tartly, 'then you can just jolly well go again!'

He stood up. She saw he was a good deal taller than she was, and it threw her, because she was five feet nine, and there were not many men, admittedly of her limited acquaintance, whom she had to look up to.

'As a matter of fact, your bag has been there a good few hours,' he told her.

Darcy tried to remember if he had carried her and her bag to bed last night. She didn't think so. 'You came to my room while I was asleep,' she accused.

'With both of us objecting to sharing your *chaste little* bed, I thought you might require something else to keep you warm.'

His look was mocking when she looked at him. And

she knew from his sarcasm that he was remembering, and not believing, her assertion that she was a virgin. Well, if he thought she was going to thank him for coming in and covering her with a quilt, then he had another think coming!

Darcy went straight to her bag, picked it up and sat on the bed with her back to him as she looked inside. The package Jane had given her to deliver was not there; she hardly expected that it would be. But every other item appeared to be there—lipstick, purse, ball-point, scribbling pad. She took up her comb, and just to show him how much his presence did not bother her, she began to drag the comb through her fine hair.

Then she discovered just how much pretence it was— for her hands started to shake when he came and stood looking down on her, saying nothing, but just standing watching her, his eyes steady on what she was doing, apparently having no aversion to observing the way her hair sprang shiningly into its natural wave.

Exasperated, as she thought he had been last night, she found him just too much. Irritably she pushed the comb out of sight in her handbag.

'Now see here, you,' she began, doubting she would have called him by his name even had she known it, 'just how long do you imagine you're going to keep me . . .'

'You mean you don't like my home?' he chopped her off.

Tight-lipped, she threw, 'I need some fresh clothes.'

'And I need a few answers,' he gritted.

It was impasse, then? He was set on believing the worst of her—the worst of every woman, she suspected. And what answers could she give him, other than the answers she had given him last night? And how could she convince him she had been speaking the truth, when her only proof that she hadn't been lying lay with Adaptable Temps? And why, for the very first time ever, had Jane inadvertently scuttled any chance she had of convincing this brute of a man, by failing to switch the answer-phone on?

'So you're determined not to confess,' said the tall glowering man, obviously thinking he had given her enough time to start talking, not a shred of mockery about him now as Darcy lifted her green-brown eyes to stare mutinously up at him.

Fleetingly, she wondered what chance she had this morning of this flint-hard man believing her if she trotted out again everything she had said last night. From the whole aggressive stance of him, she could see there was no chance.

'I'm hungry,' she snapped.

'Then we'd better go to the kitchen, hadn't we?' he returned smartly. And with his hand beneath her elbow, he had her on her feet before she could alter her mind about the needs of her stomach.

CHAPTER THREE

HER eyes, when she had been carried up the two flights of stairs they now started to descend, had been closed to the glare of light, her head buried in his shoulder, Darcy remembered with self-disgust. But now, as she tried to tug her arm out of the firm hold in which it was held, she could see the staircases were truly magnificent.

The handrail was of carved oak, very old. Immaculate wood panelling covered the walls. The stairs were wide, spiralling, covered in the lushest of warm red carpeting. That in itself told her that the twenty thousand pounds, the asking price of—what was his name?—Stoddart, had wanted wouldn't be missed.

The hard hand on her arm refused to let go, turned her to go right at the bottom of the stairs. The hall was wide, with several doors leading off it, but all doors were closed, nothing to indicate behind which door the study with that black couch lay.

Some way along the hall, she was made to go to the right again, along another hall, a shorter hall this time. Her jailer halted her to pull a door that opened outwards. It led to the kitchen, Darcy saw.

The kitchen was so large as to be vast. But her eyes had no interest in the superb fittings or kitchen machinery. Her interest lay with the kitchen door. That way must lead into a courtyard, a way out anyway. Her mind was already at work. If only she could ... A tough-sounding voice told her its owner was a thought-reader.

'The kitchen door is locked. So too are the windows, if you're fancying your chances.'

She glared at him. *He* might think he was going to keep her prisoner, but *she* knew damn well he wasn't!

41

As far as she could tell there appeared to be no one else in the house except the two of them. And since he couldn't watch her every minute of the day and night, then she was going to wait her chance—then Mr Grimface without a name wouldn't see her heels for dust.

'This place doesn't run itself,' she said, fishing, wanting confirmation that there was no one else there but the two of them as she watched while he placed bacon under the grill. 'What time do your domestic staff arrive?'

He flicked her a sideways glance, the only confirmation she received being that he saw straight through her. 'They live in.' He went back to the grilling bacon.

'But you've given them the day off?' she pressed moodily.

'A few days, actually,' he said with a pleasantness she had no belief in.

Silently she fumed. From that she gathered his servants would not be back until he contacted them.

'What about your wife?' she questioned, a spark of hope there that when his wife discovered he was keeping a young woman prisoner, she might have some influence in making him release her.

The insincere smile he threw her way would have curdled milk. 'I have no wife.' His attention went from her to the two eggs he cracked into a pan.

'That doesn't surprise me,' she said, having discerned from his intelligent face that he wouldn't miss the intimation that no woman would put up with him for long enough to marry him.

She earned herself a sour look, but didn't care as sullenly she took a few paces forward to inspect the frying pan.

'The yoke of your egg is broken,' she observed, seeing the yellow of one of the eggs was running.

Oddly, she thought she caught a glimmer of a natural smile about his mouth at her hint that he could have the egg with the broken yoke, the whole one for her.

The smile didn't last. His grim look quickly replaced it. 'Tea or coffee?' he grunted.

'I have a *choice*?'

'Coffee,' he stated, ignoring her sarcasm.

Darcy was hungry enough to put her principles behind her and eat at his table. She had eaten nothing since yesterday morning. Anyway, she reasoned, if she was going to have to sprint like fury once she had made it to the outside, she would need all the energy breakfast would provide.

Her eyes caught the kitchen clock. She saw it was midday, late for breakfast, and decided bacon and eggs were possibly the limit of his culinary expertise.

'Might I be allowed to know what you intend to do with me?' she asked when she had cleared her plate. Her courage had never felt higher; she had a full stomach to thank for that, she thought.

That was until her glance rested on his skinned knuckle, already healing over, her eyes shooting to his when he didn't answer. He had witnessed her looking at his hand, though, she saw, and then began to regret she had eaten so much when she saw his look flick to his hand, then up to her delicately shaped chin.

'You'd hit a woman!' she gasped, her courage deserting her as those hard eyes told her he would if she didn't soon start giving him the answers he wanted. And then all attempt at bravado left her. 'I've told you the truth about me,' she found herself babbling. 'Why won't you believe me?'

'You have another phone number you'd like me to try this morning?' he queried with heavy sarcasm.

'I can't understand it. Jane always switches the . . .'

'Leave it,' he ordered, and abruptly got up from the table.

Anger flared in her. It was all right for him! She was the one at her wits' end, not him. 'I've told you the truth!' she yelled, scraping back her chair, jumping to her feet ready to have a go at him.

Entirely unmoved, his glance raked her, the glint in

his eyes telling her that he still believed she was lying in her teeth.

Despondency hit her, extinguishing her spurt of temper. She tried to beat it; she couldn't afford to give up. Lord knew how Emmy was faring on her own. Yet she didn't dare tell him she was desperate to get home because she had a sometimes confused elderly lady waiting for her. Who knew, he might send those thugs around to check. Panic for Emmy hit her when she recalled the way that muscle-bound man had yanked her into that hotel room.

She bit down her panic and sought for ways to get through to this man who had cooked breakfast for them both. She tried another tack.

'I'm sorry you've had—all this trouble, I really am,' she said.

She did not like at all the way he ignored her just as though she hadn't spoken. He didn't even bother looking at her as he placed their used dishes in the sink. But she wasn't beaten yet. She went to help clear the table.

'Blackmail is a revolting business,' she went on, and, still trying to get through, 'But honestly, I haven't a clue who Stoddart is, much less what it was you wrote in that letter that he could use to . . .' Her words broke off as, startled, she saw that somehow what she had said had surprised him, she could see it in his face.

'What I . . .' His eyes were sharp on her. Then he said no more, but clamped his lips tight shut, and bent across her for the cruet, his face hidden.

She wondered what she had said that had taken him out of his stride. Then she decided that just then wasn't the time to go into it. A definite feeling was coming to her that she had dented the surface of him, minute though the dent appeared to be. She pressed on, wanting him to know how guiltless she was.

'Look, Mr . . .' she stopped, defeated that he wasn't forthcoming with his name. 'Look,' she said, trying not to get aggravated, 'why don't you call the police in to question me?' Surely that would convince him she had nothing to hide.

'You know damn well why not.'

'No, I don't,' she returned hotly.

'You aren't that thick,' he grunted, his eyes going over her as he turned from the sink.

Darcy swallowed as his eyes rested briefly on her breasts, and flicked to the shoulder she had given up trying to cover. Then his hard-eyed expression was on her face.

'The only reason blackmail ever succeeds is because the blackmailer knows full well his victim will do anything, pay any amount, to keep quiet just why it is he's being blackmailed.'

'So you think I suggested calling in the police because I know full well you can't?'

He didn't answer. But she had her answer anyway, didn't she? Hadn't he handled the matter quite satisfactorily without calling in the police? She'd like to bet it would be many a long day before Stoddart tried his hand at blackmailing anybody again.

Used to washing up with Emmy, automatically she reached for the tea towel to dry the dishes he was washing. Neither of them spoke, a grim silence hanging in the air. That was until the question that was buzzing around in Darcy's head refused to stay down any longer.

'Are you well known?' she asked, her reasoning telling her that he might be. This house, its expensive fittings, the fact that Stoddart thought he could get twenty thousand out of him without too much trouble, all pointed to his affluence.

'In certain circles.'

'So you wouldn't want the press to get hold of the fact that you've been up to no good?'

Hard eyes were on her again. 'You mean kidnapping you?'

She hadn't meant that. She had meant whatever he was being blackmailed over. But she didn't have time to tell him, for suddenly he had taken her roughly by the shoulders, his hands crushing, his expression barbaric as dangerously he warned:

'If you have any idea in your mercenary little head of selling any of this to the Sunday press, then I promise you now, you'll live to regret it!'

'I didn't mean that!' she disclaimed quickly, open-mouthed. And as his hold on her threatened to have her bones cracking, 'You're hurting me!' she wailed. 'Isn't the fact I got manhandled yesterday enough for you?'

To her further astonishment, she was instantly freed, his fury with her dying. 'Manhandled? I told them not to mark you.'

He had wanted to do that himself, she recalled. And her speech was temporarily suspended as she rolled back her sleeve and showed him the discoloration on her arm.

'How do you suppose I got that?' she asked quietly, adding for good measure, 'And a torn shirt?'

'From what I was told, it wasn't easy putting you in the back of a car to be brought here,' he told her.

And Darcy knew surprise again. Having no memory of getting her shirt torn, she guessed she had been taken out of her car coat while the doctor checked her over—where her car coat was now she didn't have a clue—but it was from the way, once he had seen the bruise on her arm, that his hand should come forward just as though he was about to soothe the livid mark that her surprise came. That was before she abruptly turned his attention back to his chores at the sink.

Knowing she must have been mistaken that the way his hand had come out as though to gently touch her bruise, Darcy was still having the devil's own work trying to fathom what to make of him.

One minute he had had her shoulders in a crushing vicelike grip, had intimated that it wouldn't put him out too much to knock her head off, yet the moment she told him he was hurting her he had let go his hold, and had even appeared to be regretful that she had, through him, collected that whopping bruise yesterday.

She put the tea towel to dry, her eyes following him

as he neatly put away the things they had used. He puzzled her, she had to admit it. He didn't look like a man who was anywhere near to being at home doing kitchen chores.

And with that thought, Darcy had to wonder then— was he a naturally tidy person, or was he putting the crockery away so that when his staff returned they would not suspect he had entertained company in their absence? Company, unlike his usual overnight companions, he didn't want them to know anything about?

She brought her mind away from him and what he did for relaxation, and looked out of the kitchen window. There *was* a courtyard out there! But, disappointed, she realised that was about all she could see. She was desperate for some sign of where she was—for all she knew, she could be in Scotland, or anywhere, miles from London.

'Mr . . .' she began, about to try and get him to tell her, then was filled with absolute frustration as it came to her that he wouldn't tell her anyway. She had his attention, she saw, unsmiling though his attention was while he waited for her to continue. But just then the frustration in her came to a head, and the question she had been about to ask vanished as, not very politely, the words burst from her, 'What the hell *is* your name?'

Unmoved, he looked levelly back, but no answer came her way. If he saw she looked ready to break a blood vessel, then he took no heed.

'Oh, damn you, then,' she snapped angrily. 'I'll call you Jasper!'

Surprise was in her once more, that he smiled then. Though she was sure it wasn't because she had reached his sense of humour that Jasper was always the villain of the piece—he just didn't have a sense of humour. But how that genuine smile altered his face, made him look more approachable. He's got super teeth, she found herself thinking, then discovered that, unmoved by her temper as he certainly was, something in her manner must have got through to him.

'Make it Neve,' he said.

'Mr Neve?' she queried, the name striking no bells in her memory as being that of anyone well known that she had heard of.

'Just Neve will do.'

For no reason, and she had nothing at all to smile about, Darcy found a smile coming from her. It curved her mouth upwards, showed where the braces she had worn as a child had done a perfect job, and had Neve staring at her for several long moments as though he thought her smile too was a definite change for the better.

Then that hard glint was back in his eyes. Aggression only was there in his face as he grated, 'Are you ready yet to admit that while Stoddart went to pick up the money, you, as his accomplice, went to deliver the goods?'

Her smile died. She hated him that for no reason he could make her lips curve a fraction. She was sure then the only reason he had smiled was in order to soften her up so she would be more receptive when he decided to have a go at her. And she damned him. And a perversity she hadn't known was in her nature chose just that very moment to want an airing.

'And if I am?' she asked impudently, then knew fear again as his face darkened and he took a step nearer. 'Though I'm not,' she said hastily, and was stammering as he checked, 'B-but I just can't th-think what you want from me. I mean, you've got your property back, haven't you?' Something she hadn't thought of before sped in. 'Or—or are you still being blackmailed?'

She was sure he wouldn't have answered, had or had not a phone started to make itself heard somewhere.

'Come with me,' he gritted, moving towards the hall door and standing there with it open, his expression saying if she was going to be tiresome he would drag her, by the hair if need be, to ensure she went with him.

Side by side they walked along the hall until he stopped at the third door down. It was the study she had last night, or rather this morning, come round in.

Because she had no choice, Darcy went into the room with him. She kept her ears open as he picked up the telephone, but pretended not to be interested as she went to the window and noted that there was nothing but green out there, not another house in sight.

She heard him say, 'Yes,' a couple of times, and, 'I told you to leave it with me,' and, 'Yes,' again. None of which made any sense, except that, although he was sounding fairly blunt, there was none of the coldness in his voice he reserved for her.

She looked to the right of the study window and saw in the distance, about a quarter of a mile away, she thought, a thick clump of trees. When she made her escape they would be ideal to hide in until she got her bearings, she thought, then wished she had been paying more attention to what the man Neve was saying, for suddenly she left her absorption with the trees on hearing him say:

'It wasn't a male accomplice.'

So whoever he was talking to must know he was being blackmailed! Well, that figured. Her brain must really have been dulled, she thought. It was obvious, now she came to think about it, since the issue involved in the blackmail was a letter. A letter had to be from some one person to another person. Had his mistress written an indiscreet letter to him? Was that what it was all about? She had noted his look of virility—it went without saying he wasn't celibate. Was his mistress a married lady? Had ... Her thoughts ceased as she heard Neve answer whatever was being said to him.

'I haven't decided yet. But that isn't your problem. Though you can help in one way.' A pause, then, 'My— house guest—was travelling light when she decided to come on here. Do what you can in the way of bringing her a change of clothes. For some reason, bearing in mind the dirty business she's engaged in, she objects to wearing yesterday's linen.'

Darcy spun round, her eyes spitting fire, and saw his

eyes flick impersonally over her. 'A size twelve, I should say,' he informed his caller, and with that, put down the phone.

There was so much Darcy wanted to fling at him, not least some sarcastic jibe that he must know something about women and then some to know anything about the way women's sizes were graded. His estimate of her being a size twelve was spot on. But as she saw the phone, an idea was born in her, and she was keeping down everything else, and voicing:

'Try Adaptable Temps again. I'm sure there'll be a reply now. Jane very often pops into the office on a Saturday.'

He looked through her. She hadn't really expected him to act on her plea anyway, she thought, annoyed that she had bothered. Everything about him said nobody led him down the garden path more than once.

The annoyance his looking through her aroused was added to when, just as though she wasn't there, he seated himself before his desk and took out his pen. He was going to work! Astounded, she stared as he pulled the papers he had been working on last night forward.

'What about *me*?'

Unconcerned, he raised his head. 'What about you?' he asked, just as if he could see nothing wrong.

'What am I supposed to do?'

'Can't you amuse yourself?'

Her eyes went to the door, but he was shaking his head even as she was suggesting, 'I could go for a walk.'

'Take a seat and keep quiet,' he instructed in no uncertain tone.

'I'll get bored.'

He smiled a smile that wasn't a smile. 'That will make two of us.'

She glowered at him. She was piqued again that he found her boring, but didn't trust him not to grab hold of her and throw her at the couch if she attempted to walk through that door.

Her eyes full of loathing she felt for him, Darcy went

to the couch and sat down, not liking him any the more
that within minutes he was immersed in his paper work,
so oblivious of her he didn't so much as once raise his
eyes.

Many thoughts went through Darcy's head as the
minutes stretched into half an hour. To start with there
had been nothing but mutiny in her soul, but as the end
of those thirty minutes neared, she discovered, looking
at that head still bent over his work, traces of silver at
his temples, and fell to wondering about the complexities
of the man who was keeping her incarcerated.

She had no way of knowing if it was usual for a
kidnap victim to be fed the midday breakfast he had
personally cooked for her. But she couldn't help wondering that he should instruct someone to bring her
something else to wear. He seemed a particularly soured
individual, she thought, and yet once or twice he had
shown her unexpected kindnesses.

It was quiet in the room, and unused to going a whole
thirty minutes without some sort of activity, she was on
the border of fidgeting, when into the silence her ears
picked up the sound of a car engine.

Not stopping to think, she was on her feet, hope in
her heart that somehow she might get whoever it was to
listen to her, to take her with them when they left. That
hope was soon vanquished, for Neve too had heard the
car and left his seat.

Without saying a word he had grasped one of her
wrists, and without stopping to wait for any argument
she might have, he had her out of the study and was
using his strength to urge her up the stairs.

It wasn't what she wanted. Half way up she gripped
her free hand round the carved oak banister, hooking
her arm through the wooden railings.

Neve let out an expletive that didn't sound too polite,
and she felt pain as, uncaring where he gripped, the
bruised part of her arm was pulled and she was hoisted
like a sack of potatoes over his shoulder.

'You great big . . .' was all she managed to yell when

she got her breath back, for the next thing she knew he had carried her to the room she had awakened in that morning and dumped her on the bed. Darcy threw him an infuriated look as she rubbed her maltreated arm.

'You asked for it,' he said shortly, his eyes leaving the fury in hers to observe the way she was rubbing her arm. Then the hard edge suddenly went from him. 'I didn't mean to hurt ...' He broke off as though he regretted the impulse to begin to apologise, that hard note back again. 'You just stay put—and keep away from the window.'

'Afraid I'll see your lady-love?' she sneered, having realised just who might be calling. And, realising something else, 'Are you afraid I'll recognise her and blab it to the Sundays?'

Involuntarily she flinched as, his manner threatening, he bent over her, a squeak she was ashamed of escaping as his hands whipped to her shoulders.

'You breathe a word of this to a living soul ...' he began, looking ready to shake her until her teeth rattled. That was until he saw her flinch back, then as if aware he was again hurting her, just as swiftly as his hands had come to her shoulders, they fell away. 'Just you— behave yourself,' he bit, then went striding to the door.

The key was already being inserted, being turned, when her temporarily subdued spirit returned. 'I'm sure as hell not going to keep away from the window!' she shouted. There was no answer, she could have saved her breath.

Going to the window did her no good at all. There was a red sports car down there, but no occupant. Not that she was interested in his line in mistresses anyway, she thought, and put her mind to better use.

The window, though fastened, unlocked easily enough. And there was a way of escape too—though she would be mad to try it. The balcony down there looked a long, long way away. The ground beneath looked rock-hard and solid too, making her mentally wince that even if she made it to the balcony, it would still leave a mighty drop to reach terra-firma.

She pulled back in, not closing the window since she intended to poke her head out again the moment *his* visitor looked like leaving. Surely another woman would see where he couldn't, or wouldn't, just how innocent of any crime she was?

Darcy spent the next ten minutes in damning people like the unknown Stoddart and his evil ways, and a couple more minutes in wondering if he felt any better than she did this morning. Then she used some more time in thinking Stoddart had certainly tried it on with the wrong man when he had tried to blackmail the man Neve.

It was the sound of the sports car roaring away that had her leaving her thoughts and jetting to the window. She blamed the fact of not being in the window position ready to call down to the woman on the fact she would have thought Neve's mistress would have stayed longer. As it was, anything she chose to shout would have been lost beneath the roar of the car. And she had no chance to recognise the woman either. All she did catch a glimpse of was blonde hair fluttering as the car sped away.

Disgruntled, she closed the window and returned to the bed, sinking down on it and stretching out, her hands to the back of her head, one knee of her long shapely legs bent in a casual attitude she was far from feeling.

She expected Neve to come and let her out straight away. But when five minutes elapsed without the sound of that key in the lock, she began to think he had been so taken up with reflections on his lady-love's visit that he had forgotten he had a prisoner upstairs. Her imagination went wild as she had visions of being allowed to rot where she lay before he remembered her existence.

Her imagination righted itself when she heard him at the door. And still determined not to be cowed, she hadn't moved from her seemingly relaxed posture when Neve entered, a paper parcel under his arm.

'And there was me thinking you had designs on my virtue,' she jibed. And just to let him know she had meant what she had shouted after him; that she hadn't kept away from the window. 'Your fancy runs to the blonde-haired of the species, doesn't it?'

He wasn't amused. She hadn't intended that he should be. Though she hadn't intended either that he should look as though it wouldn't bother him to throttle her.

'Did you recognise her?' he rapped, when she had recalled that, according to him, she was supposed to know who the female was anyway. 'Did you?' He was demanding to be answered, giving her no time to more than wonder if perhaps he had got round to thinking Stoddart hadn't told her who the lady was in case she wanted to try some little blackmailing game of her own.

'Still trying to protect the lady's doubtful good name?' she dared, angry herself that nobody appeared to care two hoots about her good name; blackmailer was a label she was tired of having hung around her neck.

'Did you?' he thundered.

And suddenly Darcy knew a terrible fear as his gigantic aggression broke in him, evidenced by the way his hands curled into tight fists, tight fists he looked ready to let fly at her with his massive strength.

Alarm rocketed when he started to advance when she still hadn't answered. 'N-no—no,' she stuttered quickly, hating that he had soon flushed out the coward in her, but too terrified of being on the receiving end of those powerful knuckles not to back down.

The fist unwound, became a sensitive long-fingered hand again. But her alarm stayed, making her wary of him. She wasn't anywhere near to trusting him, and was quaking inside when he moved to toss the paper parcel at her.

'I'll give you three minutes to change,' he ground out, his tone letting her know if she took four she would be in trouble. And with an ominous toughness there, he said through his teeth, 'Then I think you and I should have a little talk.'

With a speed that told her he was having a hard time controlling his emotions, the anger she had fired in him by her insolence, he left.

Darcy could wish the fear he had ignited in her would disappear as abruptly as him. Even as she was doing his bidding, changing into fresh underwear, a bra that fitted where it touched and was so skimpy it was positively indecent, her nerves were getting to her. She was zipping up the jeans, too short for her long legs, when panic took hold. Hurriedly she shrugged into the shirt that had come in the parcel, a paroxysm of shaking taking her as the word she had left her with, the threat behind them, drummed in her head, 'I think we should have a little talk'.

And Darcy knew desperation. He hadn't believed her before; he would not believe her now, she knew it. Not now when he had seen his girl-friend, that strong feeling of wanting to protect the blonde reinforced from seeing her, that same feeling that had had that hard fist smashing into Stoddart.

With panic rioting in her at that thought, she knew he had been ready to knock her flying when she'd been insulting about the lady's good name, that protective feeling uppermost when she had given him the impression she had seen more of the blonde than just her hair.

Near to sobbing in her fear of him, her fear of knowing that same physical violence he had meted out to Stoddart before his 'little talk' with her was over, Darcy raced to fling open the window. In her panic that balcony did not look to be so far distant.

She tried hard for common sense, but was unable to hold down panic as it was borne in on her that she just couldn't wait around for him to come, she *had* to do something.

She thought she heard him at the door, and in no time had clambered on to the windowsill—it had to be now or never. She had time for one shaky breath, and was ready.

Whether or not she would have landed safely on the

balcony below, she never found out. A bellow like that of an enraged bull sounded behind her just as she was ready to go. Her feet did leave the windowsill, but not in the direction she had planned.

Hard, iron-hard, hands were on her—gripping hands that seized hold anywhere they could grasp a hold, and she was being hauled back.

Those hands had the opppsite effect from diminishing her panic. All Darcy was aware of was that Neve had hold of her, had grabbed her with one arm firmly round her waist, while the other was part way round her, his hand clamped just as firmly on to her left breast.

She did not see then that his only intention was to get her back into the room. Her thinking haywire, all she knew was that she had not escaped, and that his hand on her breast could only mean that while his taste favoured blondes, he was not averse to females with black hair either. That the connotation she had put on the talk he wanted had been wrong. That, oh, God help her, he wanted something else entirely!

It was then that Darcy began to fight.

CHAPTER FOUR

PANICKING wildly, her feet not touching the ground, Darcy was hauled to safety.

'Let me go!' she screamed, her voice rising hysterically, hitting and kicking out as she was hurled round, buttons flying from her shirt as she struggled to be free.

'You stupid bitch,' Neve barked, 'you could have killed yourself!'

She kicked out again, her writhing wriggling movements taking him off balance, so he had to let her go. Or so she thought. But he still had hold of her by her shirt.

She was mindless then as she cannoned into a chair, sent it crashing over with a thud, to anything but that she had to get away, had to get free. She was uncaring, when quickly she released her arms from her shirt, leaving Neve hanging on to it, that there was little left to the imagination; the skimpy bra barely covered her. She wanted out—and the door was open.

Darcy never made it as far as the open door. Neve had hold of her bare arms before she could get that far, his hands transferring to her wrists as he turned her and prevented her efforts to hit him.

Panic-stricken as she was, Darcy saw his eyes go down to her heaving, inadequately covered breasts, and thought she read desire in the eyes that lifted to hers. Panic would not be controlled. 'No!' she cried, her voice hardly audible as she tried to pull free.

But he would not let her go, and she was fighting again—fighting against that piercing look in his eyes, finding her voice to scream, 'No! No!' The word 'Rape' spun round in her head so that when he picked her up and threw her on the bed, she was convinced rape was going to become a reality. It had to be. He was on the bed with her, lying over her, stilling her fighting, writhing body with his weight.

Afterwards she realised she must have gone a little crazy then. Control certainly was nowhere about as hysteria took over. Wildly she fought, a terrified screaming coming from her. Then suddenly a stinging blow to the side of her face had her breathless.

Her breath sucked in. Shock from the blow Neve had struck her set her hysterical world to rights.

'You—*hit* me!' she gasped, her breath coming painfully.

Her eyes brimming with tears, she blinked, then looked at Neve, and saw there was shock in his face too. Shock that he had actually hit her. And, calming down, she knew then without a doubt that he had never raised a hand to a woman in his life—that he never had intended to physically harm her.

'I—had to.' There was pain in him she didn't understand, as gently then, as though she was a baby, he gathered her into his arms, and a hoarse, 'Darcy,' left him.

She felt his lips on hers, not seeking or hungry as only a minute earlier she had imagined they would be, not loathesome either as she had been certain they would feel. And for no reason she could think of, almost as if they needed that gentle kiss to salve each other's pain, it just did not enter her head to struggle out of his hold. Pliant, she lay there, accepting his kiss. He was still gentle with her when his lips left her quiescent mouth, no word being spoken as he looked down into her liquid eyes.

Then he moved slightly, glancing down to where her breasts were still rising and falling from her exertions. And the next time he kissed her, his kiss was different.

She had felt his warmth before, but now there was a growing heat in him. His lips left her mouth, to kiss her

shoulders, her breasts, and Darcy thought it must be
because she was too stunned by what had happened,
what *was* happening, to do what good sense was trying
to tell her—to resist.

His mouth captured hers again, and she knew her
thinking must be all over the place still. Because she
could do nothing when he drew a sweet longing from
her, other than put her arms around him, and meet his
kiss with a need of her own.

A voice, not hers, not his, was another shock—a
shock that went a long way to bringing her to her senses.
The voice came from the doorway, had her eyes leaping
there as Neve raised his head, pink colouring every
visible part of her.

'Well, well, Neve,' said the tall good-looking young
man who stood there, unable to see more of her than
her pink face and naked arms, which were still around
the man who lay covering her, 'I don't recall you ever
bringing your—playmates—into the house before. Is
this . . .'

'Get out, Blair,' Neve told him bluntly, without turning to see who it was, already his hand at the side of her
face. Just as though he was trying to protect her from
view, Darcy thought with what coherency she had left.
'And close the door after you.'

'Pardon me for intruding,' said the man called Blair,
a laugh in his voice as he did as he was bidden.

Shame hit her the moment he had gone. Her face scarlet,
she found her voice, and hissed, 'Get off me!' Then she
discovered Neve too had gone off whatever idea had been
in his head. Without a word he rolled off the bed.

Darcy sat up. The loathing that should have been in
her before, only which unfortunately had been nowhere in sight, surged upwards, and stayed there. It
was there in her eyes as she looked at him. Loathing
for herself as well as him as she saw distaste in him
as he looked down at the tarty-looking bra that just
about covered the pink tips of her breasts and no
more.

'I didn't choose the underwear,' she said hotly. And, wanting to hurt, 'It's your lady-friend's taste, not mine.' She saw that hard look come back to him on being reminded of why she had been overnight in his house without so much as a toothbrush of her own, and was on the receiving end of his stinging, wounding, comment:

'She probably thought—*rightly*—the game you're in, that you were the sort of tramp who would appreciate such a garment.'

Darcy felt ill, sick in her stomach. His 'She probably thought—*rightly*' could only mean he was of the opinion, since she had responded the way she had to his kisses, that she was some sort of tramp.

'I didn't . . .' she tried, but got no further. For sourly, as if just looking at what he could see of her breasts offended him, he was snarling:

'Cover yourself up! '

Her eyes searched feverishly for her shirt; his suggestion was the best she had so far heard. But it was Neve who found it on the floor, throwing it at her as though to come near her, to have to touch her was more than he could stomach.

Losing no time, Darcy had her shirt about her, hugging it to her, since there wasn't a button left on it. But although he wasn't approaching the bed, she was overwhelmingly conscious of him watching her, and wanted his attention anywhere but on her, not wanting herself to remember the way she had been with him, the way he could make her feel.

'Who was that who came in?'

Neve moved away at her question and went to stand over by the window. 'My brother,' he said, when she had thought she was going to have to run for her answer. And while that was sinking in, he was commanding, 'Come here.'

Though she did not see why she should obey any of his orders, the quiet authority in him had her leaving the bed, going half way to the window before she stopped. Stopped, and was wary of him.

'I said, come here.'

He had turned, angrily, the hand he stretched out as if to pull her the rest of the way having her backing out of range. She saw from the way his jaw suddenly jutted that he had read that she was afraid he intended to take her in his arms again.

'You idiot!' he exploded. 'What happened just now was entirely—unscripted. I didn't know it was going to happen.' With an effort he reined in his anger, then told her tersely, 'It won't happen again. I . . .' He broke off as still she refused to come any closer.

'Look,' he said, and she knew she was severely testing his patience, for all he seemed to be mastering it, 'I didn't expect it to happen, didn't expect to get the shock of my life by coming in to find you in the middle of a suicidal jump. It—threw me,' he admitted. 'I had to act fast. Then you went berserk—you could have tried for the window again, and I still didn't have time to think. Had I done so I should have known that if I had your body beneath mine, quiet at last, your lovely tear-filled eyes looking reproachfully up at me, natural chemistry might rear its head.'

Had she gone berserk? Probably, she had to own, and found herself confessing, 'I thought you were going to rape me,' and had to wrinkle her brow as that confession left her. For if he was in any way apologising for what had happened, then, as the words left her, it sounded to her just as though she was apologising too. And she had nothing to apologise for!

Neve shook his head. But somehow she knew that to rape her had never been in his mind even before that gesture. And when, quietly, he said, 'Come here now,' Darcy found her feet moving forward.

At the window she looked to where he pointed—not to the balcony, but to where the driveway met the edge of a lawn. So what was so remarkable about a pile of scaffolding poles? She very soon discovered.

'The balcony below is unsafe—the workmen will be here next week.'

She swallowed, and couldn't hold back the shudder that went through her. She saw then that when he had said her jump would have been suicidal, he had been speaking the truth. Even if she had made it that far in one piece, which was very debatable, the sudden force of even her light weight on an unsafe balcony could well have had it collapsing.

'I would have broken my neck, wouldn't I?' she whispered. Then, getting over that shaken moment, she realised she was being far too meek and mild. It was all his fault she had been going to try it anyway. 'I was upset,' she said, her voice firmer. And with her anxieties about Emmy gnawing away again, she snapped, 'I wanted—want to get back to London.'

His tone had toughened too. 'You're saying you're so desperate to see Stoddart you'd risk your neck again?' He turned, a furious glint in his eyes. 'Even though you know what would happen if you went through that window?'

'I've told you,' she spat, 'I don't know Stoddart. I'd never even heard of him until . . .'

'Are you in love with him?' he grated, going off on some tack of his own, she was sure.

'I don't *know* him,' she repeated heatedly. 'Can't you get that into your . . .'

'Are you in love with anyone?' he asked—to her mind a question that had got nothing to do with any of it.

But she was growing angry too. He wasn't believing she didn't know Stoddart, and it was a sure-fire thing he wouldn't believe her if she told him she didn't have time to go out and meet anyone it might be possible for her to fall in love with. Any spare time she had when not looking after Emmy and keeping her company was spent in swotting to make herself an all purpose temp, so that she would be able to accept any job that came her way.

'Well,' he insisted, his patience at an end, 'are you?'

'It's none of your damned business,' she said witheringly.

He didn't like her answer. But she was past caring what he liked. She wanted to go home. She had never felt so confused in her life, and wanted to be back with Emmy who loved her, wanted to be where, for all Emmy often muddled things up, life seemed to be sane. She looked from him to the window, her thoughts on the balcony. It just wasn't on, and she knew it.

'You're not thinking of giving a repeat performance?' harshly hit her ears.

'You care if I break my neck?'

'On my property, yes.'

'Then let me go.'

'You'll stay here until I decide what's to be done with you.'

Darcy let out a furious breath. 'I wish you'd hurry up and make up your mind, then,' she snapped. And, no longer afraid of him, 'A pity you haven't a dungeon you can lock me in!'

He fixed her with a grim look. 'Are you going to behave yourself?'

'Me, behave *myself*!'

'Are you going to keep away from the window—or do I have to tie you to the bed?' he asked, and looked as though he meant it.

'Kinky yet,' Darcy derided, determined not to be put down. Then derision left her, for, so suddenly she couldn't believe it, his grim expression left him, and she could have sworn a smile was sternly suppressed.

But he was waiting for her answer, and she knew it was one answer he was determined to have before he left. And she wanted him to leave, wanted to be alone. She needed to be by herself to try and sort out why she

had so meekly submitted to his kisses instead of trying
to brain him as she should have done.

'I'll give you my word I won't try any acrobatics, on
condition that you keep your hands to yourself,' she
said, her chin coming up.

'Hands to myself?' he repeated, just as though he
didn't know what she meant. Though on reflection,
she couldn't recall—except when he had tried to control her—that his hands had in any way roved her
body.

She coloured, but that didn't stop her from bringing
out, 'I object to being pawed about!'

'You should get to be so lucky,' he drawled, his eyes
going insolently down the front of her.

'Oh, get out!' she said, suddenly weary, avoiding the
narrowing of his eyes by going over to the bed and sitting down. 'I value my life more than to try being a sky-
diver without a parachute.' And, not looking at him to
see what he was going to make of her next line, 'Just
leave my bread and water outside the door. The less I
see of you the better I shall like it!'

The door crashed. The key turned in the lock. Darcy
lay down, and her mind went straight to the scene that
had been enacted, starting from the moment Neve had
come in and seen her about to take a header through
the window.

Undoubtedly his quick action had saved her life.
Though since because of his imprisonment of her she
had been stewed up enough, panicky enough, to try for
that balcony anyhow, she didn't think he deserved any
thanks for that.

She faced then that she must have momentarily
become unhinged to be mad enough to think she
might land safely. She had, she supposed, been semi-
hysterical even before she had felt his hand on her
breast. And, reluctantly, she was forced to admit, to
slap her had been about the best way to bring her out
of her hysteria. Though remembering he had looked
shocked too that he had actually hit her, she had to

admit also that, vile though he was, there was something in him that disliked intensely everything he had had to do.

Serve him right, she thought a moment later. It wasn't her fault his passion for a married lady—and she had to be married, didn't she?—had got him on the sticky end of a blackmail plot. He had no right either kissing her the way he had when he was so involved with the blonde.

But when it came to analysing the way he had had her responding to him, she was hard put to discover how it had come about. She didn't like him, had felt hate for him more than any other emotion. Yet lord knew what would have happened if his brother hadn't walked in. Though she was sure, she thought quickly, it wouldn't have gone too far. She was positive of that—which in no way explained the way he had had her kissing him back.

It had to be that he was an expert in that field, she decided firmly. She had been kissed before. In fact, before her parents had died and she and Emmy had come to London, there had been one or two boy-friends, though none of them had made her feel the way Neve had, nagged a little voice that wouldn't stay quiet. And she had *liked* those boy-friends from her adolescence.

It was several hours before she saw Neve again. At some time during the afternoon she had fallen asleep, but she knew he had been in to check on her, because on one of the pale blue chairs there was a man's shirt, neatly folded as though for whoever did his ironing it was a labour of love.

Somehow she couldn't see the blonde ironing his shirts. She was probably good in other departments, she thought sourly, shrugging away that she didn't like the thought. The shirt, though, Neve having seen that she couldn't spend her time in his company with her arms hugging the front of her to keep her buttonless shirt together, was another example of some semblance of kindness in him, she thought begrudgingly.

Either that, or the fact that he found her tatty appearance too much for his refined taste, she thought, sourness back with her again that he had forgotten his distaste long enough to kiss her as though he wanted her, hadn't he?

She wondered why her mind kept going back to that scene. Why she couldn't get from her mind that shocked, regretful look, after he had hit her. Oh, to hell with him, she thought, and was fretting again about Emmy, the other source of her thoughts when she hadn't been sleeping. If only she could get to a phone, tell her not to worry, that she'd be home soon.

Her stomach was letting her know it would be glad of the bread and water she had flung at Neve that he could leave outside her door, when her ears caught the sound of footsteps. She braced herself to see him again when she heard the key in the lock.

'You're awake at last,' was his greeting as he stepped inside the room.

'Been checking every hour on the hour, have we?'

'When you're ready, we'll go and eat,' he said, her sarcasm not touching him as he picked up the shirt and handed it to her.

Darcy left the bed. She would love to have told him what he could do with his shirt, but compressed her lips as she walked airily past him to the bathroom.

What a sketch! she thought some minutes later—jeans way above her ankles, the shirt Neve had given her pushed down into her pants, the sleeves rolled back many times. At least he wasn't wearing a dinner jacket, she thought whimsically, clearly remembering how well he looked in his well cut beige slacks and donkey brown cashmere sweater.

'Will I do to grace your table?' she asked, coming out of the bathroom.

'You'd look good in anything, and you know it,' was his reply. And she couldn't deny, however much she

wanted to, the flutter that happened inside at his compliment, for all she offered a mocking:

'Now, now, Neve dear, don't get fresh!'

On the way downstairs she recalled the way when,
after he had slapped her, Neve had called her by her
first name. Up until then it had been Miss Alexander,
all very formal and proper. That he had slapped her
must have so shaken his equilibrium that he had called
her Darcy—it had to have done, didn't it? Which must
mean that he thought of her as Darcy, and not Miss
Alexander.

She had no idea what that meant, or if it meant
anything at all. One thing was for sure, though, if she
knew his surname she would use that and no other.
Which put in her mind the idea that she wouldn't ever
call him by his first name again. It was much too personal—and they had been more than personal enough
in her view.

As they passed the study Darcy noted that the door
was open. And although she was by now familiar with
the room, all that really registered in that brief
glimpse, as Neve led her kitchenwards, was that a
telephone stood there on the desk just crying out to
be used.

She had to get to that phone, she thought, somehow
she had to get to that phone. Even as Neve was pulling out a chair for her at the kitchen table she was
trying to think up some way of getting into that study
and being by herself to make that all-important call to
Emmy.

Bitterness welled up that because of that tall brute the
dear old lady must be suffering mental anguish. And
there was only acid in her when she saw that just two
place settings had been laid.

'No little brother Blair?' she enquired, determined
to needle him if she could. 'Or did he refuse to eat in
the servants' quarters?' She saw she was getting to
him and carried on chipping away. 'Wouldn't you prefer
to eat in the dining room with him? I promise not to

try and pick the lock on the kitchen door,' she lied.

'Like hell you wouldn't!'

And she had thought she had niggled him, she thought, giving up as the smile that broke from him lightened his face briefly.

'Blair is out,' he informed her. 'And you'll have to forgive eating in the kitchen. It's where the food is . . .'

'And it's beneath you to carry the goodies into the dining room.'

'Shut up and eat,' she was told. And she smiled, because she *had* niggled him.

'Certainly, big brother,' she said sweetly. 'What delight has my jailer prepared?'

'You're plucky, I'll say that for you.'

'We blackmailers are,' she said, and knew she had gone too far. But he managed to hang on to his temper long enough to place a bowl of soup in front of her and not upend it over her head as had looked likely.

Grateful for small mercies, Darcy did as she was bid. She shut up and ate. Though as the meal progressed and Neve got over the ill humour she had provoked, she was to learn that it was not to be a silent meal, although she was cutting into a luscious steak before he said another word.

'You said you live alone,' he remarked suddenly, his eyes studying the clarity of the wine in his glass.

For a moment or two she had no rejoinder to make. Alert to danger as she was, every sense told her he mustn't know about Emmy. He could be ruthless—oh yes, he could be ruthless. She knew it, even having seen a gentler side to him. Emmy must not be dragged into this.

'That's right,' she said casually, the moment already gone when she could plead to his short supply of gentleness, maybe understanding, and tell him about Emmy.

'Stoddart isn't planning to move in with you?'

That man's name again! She felt like screaming at

him that he still wouldn't believe she didn't know the wretched man.

'If ever I do meet a man of that name, I'll give him your regards,' she said tightly, throwing him a look of aggravation. Her glance fell away as she saw he had done with studying his wine and those dark piercing eyes were now on her, taking her apart.

Leaving the subject of Stoddart, he then set out on a different course, determined, it seemed, to know everything there was to know about her.

'So you don't live with your parents?'

'My parents are dead.'

She would have left it there, but flicking a glance at him she read in his eyes that he was waiting for more, that regardless of any pain it might cause her, that short statement wasn't sufficient.

'They died four years ago,' she said flatly, not wanting to dwell on the subject of her parents' deaths, a subject that might show some vulnerability in her when she needed both her mental and physical strength against him. She thought that sentence neatly closed the conversation.

'When you were eighteen?'

So he *had* done the simple calculation on her age from her driving licence. She nodded, wanting to leave it there.

'They died together?' he probed, making her wonder, in view of his remark about her suicidal attempt at escape, if he thought her whole family were unhinged, if her parents had formed a suicide pact.

'They were killed in a train crash while on holiday abroad,' she said, beginning to grow inflamed by his ceaseless probing.

'No brothers or sisters?' he enquired, relieving some of her tension.

'No relatives at all,' she answered.

'So you're all alone in the world?'

Except for Emmy, but he wasn't going to know about her. 'Yes,' she muttered, and felt at her most vulnerable just then.

'You have friends, of course, men-friends?'

'I live in a flat, not a nunnery,' she said flippantly, and saw he didn't like her flippant attempt to rid herself of feeling weak and weepy.

'How did you come to work at the agency?' he asked tersely.

'I . . .' she began, then saw something he had either overlooked or just hadn't been aware of. 'You believe me? That I work for the agency?' The feeling of wanting to burst into tears rapidly disappeared, her voice eager, her whole face alight. 'You believe the agency I told you of actually exists?'

And while he said nothing, but just sat watching the life come to her eyes, the animation that was suddenly there, she pressed on, urgently now.

'Give that number another ring. I'm sure Jane will have switched the recorder on. I can't think how she came to forget. We're desperate for work, I'm . . .' She had been going off at a tangent, and felt like a pricked balloon, when Neve broke in cynically;

'So desperate you'll take on any job, whether it be legal or illegal?'

Darcy stood up. Her appetite had been filled, but had it not been, she would have got up just the same. 'I'd like to go back to my cell,' she threw at him, the hope that had her tongue running away with her hit firmly on the head by his caustically dropped out remark.

It appeared he had had enough of her too. 'You have no objection if I escort you, I'm sure,' he said with all the charm of a perfect host.

Darcy marched out before him, hoping it took him until midnight to do the pile of washing up on the draining boards. But once out of the kitchen, her footsteps slowed. She could see the study door. Oh, why had she lost her temper? Had she not done so she would have had many more minutes to plan how she was going to get to the phone.

They were passing the study when her footsteps

faltered. And because Neve was so close, she bumped into him. Then before she could move a mile away, she felt his steadying hand on her arm, heard him say, 'Are you all right?' and on that instant, a plan was with her.

She leant against him, made her body go limp. 'I feel—dizzy,' she murmured, clutching at his sweater.

She felt his arm come about her, and thanked her lucky stars then that Neve was a man of action. Without wasting a second he had her through the open study door, had her seated, a hand on the back of her head, and was pushing it down between her knees.

Her hand was trembling when his came and gripped it in what might have been a comforting hold. She knew he felt her trembling, hoped he was concerned and would think it was because her nerves were shot, her 'fainting' attack all part and parcel of the trauma she was going through. The last thing she wanted him to know was that her trembling was caused by nothing other than excitement that if everything went well, she would soon be talking to Emmy.

A soft moan escaped her as she made the effort and pulled her head up. 'You look flushed,' Neve observed.

'Probably the blood gone to my head,' she whispered, still hanging on to his hand.

'How do you feel now? Still dizzy?'

'N-no. I feel—hot.'

It wasn't a lie. But she saw him look at her suspiciously, and knew fear that he had rumbled her.

'You want me to open a window?' he asked, an edge coming to his voice.

So that was it! He thought the moment the window was open she would be attempting to dive through it. Fat chance. He'd bring her down in a rugger tackle without thinking twice.

'What . . .?' she asked, just as if she wasn't right there with him. Then, licking dry lips, 'C-could I have a drink of water?' and chancing her all, she made as though to move off the chair and try to stand up. 'I'll get it.'

She was pushed back down again. She hid her elation

by lowering her eyes as Neve said, his voice losing its harshness, 'You sit quiet for a while. I won't be long.'

Take as long as you like, she thought, and, every second vital, had the phone off its rest the moment he vanished, and was trying to control her fingers as she dialled.

Emmy must have been near the phone, she thought, sending up a silent thanks to her guardian angel, for after the second ring she heard Emmy answer the phone in the way she always did.

Tears were in Darcy's eyes as she heard Emmy's, 'Hello.'

'Emmy, it's me, Darcy,' she said, gulping down tears.

'Oh, hello dear. You shouldn't have bothered ringing.'

'Emmy, I . . .' was as far as she got, before her mother's old nanny was saying:

'How's Jane, dear?'

And she knew then Emmy was going through another of her vague patches. 'She's fine, love,' she said. 'But . . .'

'You stay with her,' said Emmy, her voice warm and loving, so that Darcy had to swallow tears again. It came to her that she must think she and Jane were out on some job together.

'Emmy, Emmy dear,' she said gently, forgetful that she should be hurrying with this call, her way being never to hurry Emmy having grown over the last few years, 'what I'm ringing for is to tell you not to worry if I'm not home for a few days.'

'Oh, I won't, Darcy. I understand,'

Dear Emmy, Darcy thought, and wondered if she would confuse her more if she added anything to what she had aready said.

'I'll see you as soon as I can, darling,' she said—and then she was squealing with fright.

For, from nowhere, a long cashmere-sleeved arm had suddenly appeared. Her last word of 'darling' still hung in the air when violently the phone was snatched from her, and she was staring into the furious eyes of the man she knew only as Neve.

Looking ready to divide her from her breath, he placed the phone to his ear; but Emmy had already hung up. Darcy watched, fear in her again as the phone went crashing on its cradle. Her eyes wide, she saw the way the glass of water he held was banged on the desk, and as he turned his attention to her, never had she seen him more angry.

CHAPTER FIVE

'YOU scheming bitch!' His wrath broke over her head, causing Darcy to hastily put some space between them, ready for flight. 'You scheming, conniving bitch! You weren't feeling faint at all, were you?'

She hadn't been, but in the face of his furious anger, she was ready to wilt now. She went to retreat further, then suddenly she was as angry as him. What was she— a jellyfish?

'No, I wasn't feeling faint,' she said, holding her ground. 'And you deserve to be duped anyway. I've told you and told you I'm innocent, but you won't believe me. You're keeping me here against my will, so—so every chance I get I shall scheme against you.'

She saw his eyes glint dangerously that she was standing up to him, as he demanded, 'Who were you phoning?'

'Afraid it was the police?' she jeered, and did retreat then when he took an angry step forward.

'Do you usually call policemen "darling"?' he grated, then seemed to have control of his anger—he wasn't coming any nearer, thank goodness.

And for one idiotic moment she had the crazy idea he was more put out that she had called someone darling, than from the fact she had tricked him. She threw that idea out of the window. But her own anger had abated a little after its limited spurt; that his appeared to be now in check aided her courage.

'What's it to you?' she asked, refusing to be browbeaten, though she had to own she wouldn't have minded had he decided to push her down into a chair again; her legs were feeling decidedly shaky. Especially when, enraged by her pert answer, his anger reared again, and he thundered:

'Was it Stoddart?'

'Oh, for crying out loud!' she sighed, and had to control her anger riding again to meet his, for surely there'd be murder committed soon, and she didn't fancy herself as the victim. 'I've told you repeatedly,' she said, striving for calm, 'that I don't know anybody called Stoddart.' And from nowhere came the name of the man who had sent her on his vile errand, the name she had forgotten, dropping into her head. 'The man who engaged the agency's services was called Townsend.' And, forestalling him, 'And I wasn't ringing *him* either. I don't know him, have never met him.'

'You were phoning some other boy-friend,' he accused, making her think for a moment she had got him off the Stoddart tack, until he said, 'You run more than one boy-friend at a time?'

'I wasn't ringing a boy-friend.'

'You call every man "darling"?'

'I have a few less endearing names for you,' she couldn't help retorting.

For long furious seconds they glared at each other, then he was demanding, 'Are you going to tell me who you were calling?'

'No, I am not,' she told him in no uncertain fashion—and had to suffer those dark eyes burning into her for several seconds longer. Then he was breathing deeply, mastering the ire she had aroused. He growled, when she had been expecting anything but what he said:

'Make yourself scarce—go to your room, and stay there.'

Not liking arguments, fighting, something inside Darcy objected to being sent away like some misbehaving schoolgirl. And, illogical as she knew it was, particularly when she knew his anger was only just being held down, a furious eruption promising, when she knew it would be wiser to do as he ordered, she just had to stay and have one last jibe.

'Can I have the key to my room?' And at the question there in the narrowing of his eyes, 'I object to you coming in when I'm asleep.'

'You're in no position to object to anything I choose to do,' he replied, his voice suddenly so silky, she just knew he was remembering the way they had lain close on that bed and kissed, oblivious to anything but the feelings that had ignited when their lips had met.

She swallowed. She was a jelly-fish after all—but not without an attempt to sting. 'All the more reason why my door should be locked from inside, wouldn't you say?' she managed. And trying for sarcasm, for suddenly she wasn't feeling very brave at all, 'We mustn't have you coming to my room and doing something you would never afterwards forgive yourself for, must we?'

She didn't miss the way his jaw clenched. Nor did she hang about when, his voice dangerously quiet, his knuckles showing white on balled fists, he advised, 'Go to your room, Darcy. I can assure you you'll be the one to have something to regret if you don't.'

She managed to keep her head held high as she went. Useless to try the front door on her way—Neve would hear her, would catch her, and she still felt pale from his parting unveiled threat. The quiet way he had spoken, that thin covering of control—far more terrifying than his furious anger—had her knowing he would show her no mercy if he heard so much as the handle on the front door rattle.

Her fear of him quietened down when she had been in her room for some ten minutes. But she still felt the threat of him, and knew it wasn't just plain cowardice. Her instincts of self-preservation had never been more alert.

As yet her door wasn't locked—but he was out there somewhere. One step outside her door, she thought, the whole nightmare of the hours since she had arrived at that hotel in Banbury gathering together in several despairing minutes, and he would be ready to finish off what had started off in this very room as a gentle kiss of remorse for hitting her.

She knew that some time soon she would hear him insert the key in the lock, would be locked in until he decided to let her out, and felt then too beaten to try to do anything about it.

Because she couldn't take thinking of Neve, or what could so nearly have happened if she hadn't had the good sense to leave the study, Darcy turned her mind in the direction of Emmy.

She was still somewhat amazed that the dear soul hadn't sounded anywhere near to being demented with worry as she had expected to hear her. But she could only be glad about that, for the first time ever finding comfort in that Emmy was going through one of her bouts of being confused. She had sounded well and happy. She just hoped with everything in her that she stayed that way until she could get back to her.

Wearily Darcy looked at the door, tiredness added to the defeat of her spirit. Perhaps it would be better if she got some rest, she thought. A few hours' sleep and she was sure her spirit, bruised by what she had seen as Neve's diabolical intent on her person, would return full flow. Tomorrow she wouldn't be scared of him. Tomorrow she intended to give him hell for making her the nervous wreck she had become.

It was daylight when Darcy opened her eyes. And it was there, the spirit she wanted. It had woken with her, so that just let Mr Big, Mr Neve No-name try terrifying her today, and he would soon see what she was made of!

She went to the bathroom, and because the shirt of his was the most decent of the three at her disposal, after her wash, along with jeans that looked as though they weren't on friendly terms with her shoes, so far apart were they, she put it on. Then for ten minutes she sat on her bed waiting for him to come and let her out.

She hadn't heard him lock her in last night, she mused, and went to the door to try the handle, knowing full well before she got there that it would be locked. He was thorough, her jailer. She turned the handle. Then after one moment of disbelief, she stared in amazement. The door had opened!

Excitement sped in. He had forgotten to lock her in! It was still early—he could still be in his bed, could still be asleep!

Darcy wasted only enough time to dash back for her handbag. Then trying not to hurry too much, afraid some careless movement would have her making even the faintest noise and so disturb him, she hastened down the stairs.

Her palms were sweating when she reached the front door, sufficient light there for her to see that Neve had been uncommonly careless. The front door was not bolted. Perhaps he was tired, she thought. He'd have had to keep on his toes to see she didn't escape. He had probably not slept at all the previous night.

What was she worrying her head about that for anyway? she thought, wiping her moist hands down the sides of her jeans, those same hands going to release the doorcatch. With a bit of luck he would sleep for another hour yet, she could be a couple of miles away before then, maybe even be further if she could hitch a lift.

Her heart was in her mouth as the door moved back on its hinges. Then fear panicked her that she might at this stage, with escape so near, feel that familiar hand on her shoulder. That thought was enough to have her streaking through the door, leaving it standing wide open, the thought touching, that she would love to see his face when he saw it and realised that the bird had flown.

Elated, she ran on to the drive, then stopped, hardly daring to believe her luck. There on the drive, a black Mercedes some yards in front, stood her car!

The last time she had seen it had been when she had parked it at that hotel in Banbury. One of those two tough guys must have followed the car she had been brought in with it, she reasoned, though she didn't care at all how it had got there. It was there, and that was the thing. And if memory served, she had pulled in to fill up with petrol just before Banbury. She had a whole tankful; all she had to find out now was where the dickens she was.

Inside her car, not daring to close the door until she had the engine roaring into life, Darcy opened her bag for her car keys. Her first quick search revealed nothing. But, her elation fast fading, she still would not let herself believe that whoever had driven her car here hadn't had the decency to return her car keys to her bag.

So intent was she on rummaging through her bag, refusing to admit that she couldn't remember not seeing the keys when she had checked the contents yesterday, she almost shot through the roof when a smooth, cool voice enquired sardonically:

'Going somewhere?'

Her head spun round to the open door, her eyes going wide. For there, her car keys dangling between finger and thumb, stood Neve.

She couldn't even rant and rave at him. Her disappointment floored her. Dumbly she stared at him, and knew then he had never for a moment slackened in his duty to keep her prisoner.

Well, he'd have to drag her from her car screaming, because she wasn't going back into that house voluntarily, she thought, knowing that was his intention. And she didn't need his sarcastic:

'Discovered where you are yet?'

She could be in another country as far as she knew, although since she had been able to dial Emmy without any hold-ups last night, she hoped that meant she was still in England.

'No,' she answered sullenly.

Then she had the shock of her life—and just didn't believe it, when he handed over her car keys and said, 'I'll lead the way.'

She didn't trust him, but took the keys he offered because she wanted them. But still she didn't trust him.

'You're letting me go?' she asked suspiciously.

'The main road is a few miles off the beaten track—it's better you follow me.' He raised one quizzical eyebrow. 'I assume you wish to reach London without taking too many wrong turns.'

'How far away is London?' she asked warily.

'About thirty miles.'

If he really was letting her go she could be back with Emmy in an hour! But was he letting her go? Or was this some dreadful game he had dreamt up for his own amusement? Treading warily, she asked:

'You now believe I'm innocent? You believe Adaptable Temps exist?'

The sardonic look left him. 'I've known Adaptable Temps are bona fide since I rang and heard their recording yesterday morning,' he admitted to her astonishment.

Anger soared in her then, and she was no longer treading carefully as she spat out, 'And you've kept me prisoner since then! Even after you found out I'm entirely free of guilt!'

The look that came to him, the scepticism in him, had her anger going off the boil. 'I said I discovered the *agency* was bona fide,' he told her cuttingly.

'Which means,' she said, having no trouble in following him, 'that you still think I'm in league with this Stoddart man.' And, her grey matter having woken fully alert, 'You think between us we planned to use the agency so that if I got caught I would have a watertight story?'

He didn't answer. But she wanted an answer. Even when she didn't see why she should want him to believe her after what he had put her through, she still wanted an answer.

'You're letting me go, yet you still think I'm a partner in a blackmail plot?' she tried again.

He straightened away from the door, but not before she had seen the ruthless look that had entered his eyes. 'I know where to find you if you try to pull anything like this again,' he said, giving her the only answer he intended. And just before he slammed the door shut on her, 'Follow me.'

She watched him stride to the car in front, hating him for what he thought she was. Silently she called him a cynical swine, but that didn't make her feel any better. Not that she valued his good opinion, she thought. He meant nothing to her. It was just that being a law-abiding citizen, she was offended that anyone should so firmly believe that she wasn't.

His car started up and she set hers in motion, ready to drive straight round him, across his immaculate lawns if need be, if this was some amusement he was delighting in with no real intention of letting her go.

They were half a mile from the house when she saw a signpost pointing in the direction of the way she had come. Well, Cornthorpe was a village she hoped never to see again, she thought, watchful then of everything that went on up in front.

After many twists and turns, roads she might have gone blindly along had Neve not been leading the way, they came to some crossroads. There he halted the Mercedes and started to walk back to her. But Darcy had seen the signposts and knew then in just which direction she had to go.

He was about ten yards from her when she put her foot down, had roared away, leaving him looking after her. She was thankful it was so early in the morning, no traffic about, as she belted over the crossroads, luckily not meeting anything coming either from right or left. The last sight she had of Neve was to see him standing watching her. And all she could think then was good riddance, she'd seen the last of him.

It was still early when she reached London, and although it was Sunday there was a fair amount of traffic about. She had dreaded Neve staying on her tail all the way there. She had been unable to relax for the first few miles after she had shot off, had been afraid even then the Mercedes would come up alongside and edge her into the side of the road where he would say something like, 'And now we'll go back to Cornthorpe.'

But he hadn't followed her. Though it wasn't until she had parked her car and had her car coat under her arm—discovered on the floor at the back, obviously thrown there by one of those thugs—and was pushing her key into her flat door, that she fully believed that at last she was free.

Emmy, always up early regardless of what day it was, her ears still sharp, must have heard her, for by the time Darcy had called, 'Emmy, it's me!' and had the door closed, she was already coming along the small passageway towards her, looking so normally just her dear Emmy that Darcy was afraid she was the one who was going to break down in tears.

'Oh, Emmy,' she cried, 'I'm so glad to see you!'

'I'm glad to see you too, dear,' said Emmy. And before Darcy could begin to enquire into her health or how she had fared while she was away, she was going on, 'I expect you're tired after being at the hospital all this time. You go and relax in the sitting room while I make you a nice cup of tea.'

Hospital? Darcy followed her into the kitchen, wanted to put the kettle to boil herself, but aware of Emmy's independent spirit, restrained herself while she thought up the most tactful way to question her on this idea she had in her head that for some reason she had been staying at the hospital.

'How's the little lad this morning?' asked Emmy before anything very tactful had presented itself.

'You mean . . .'

'Little Edward. You're more tired than I thought,' stated Miss Emsworth, giving Darcy a thorough scrutiny from her faded blue eyes. 'And where on earth did you get those clothes, child?' she asked sternly. Then, suddenly smiling warmly, 'You always were fairly fastidious—when you left your mud pie days behind you. I expect you got someone at the hospital to kit you out with something.'

'Er—yes,' Darcy mumbled, her mind darting all over the place.

By the sound of it something had happened to Jane's son Edward. Oh, poor Jane! She hoped it was nothing serious, though with Emmy thinking she had stayed all weekend at the hospital keeping Jane company, it didn't sound very good.

'I'm just going to make a quick phone call,' she told her, trying to keep the urgency she was feeling from her voice.

'I'll bring the tea in when it's made,' nodded Emmy.

Quickly Darcy went into the sitting room, at this stage not wanting to ask Emmy which hospital little Edward was in, seeing complicated explanations ensuing from any such question. Though she would have to ask if Jane wasn't home. She would have to go to the hospital and offer what support she could, if Jane was there, and Edward seriously ill.

'Jane!' she said on hearing her friend's voice. 'I'm so sorry I haven't been in touch before.' This just wasn't the moment to tell her about the terrible hours she had spent since they had seen each other. Those hours must have been more than terrible for Jane if little Edward . . .

'That's all right,' she heard her friend say. 'I've been at the hospital most of the time, so you probably wouldn't have got me anyway. I did try to get you on Friday night, but with Miss Emsworth all excited about her holiday, we seemed to be getting our wires crossed. Though I think I did eventually get through to her that Edward had been involved in an accident and was in a coma.'

'Oh, Jane, I'm so sorry!' Darcy's sympathy was all for her. What she had said about Emmy thinking she was going on holiday when she wasn't, was something that could be sorted out later. 'How is Edward this morning?' she enquired, knowing Jane would have been in touch with the hospital on waking, if indeed the poor girl had been able to sleep.

'I've not long been back home, actually, he came out

of his coma in the small hours. Though . . .' Jane's voice broke for a second before she found sufficient control to go on, 'he's still very poorly, poor lamb.'

For several minutes more they talked about Edward, Emmy coming in with a tea tray and some toast, Darcy willingly offering to go to the hospital with Jane on her next visit.

'It would be a help if you could stay at home and take any phone calls,' said Jane. 'Everything about the business went from my mind the moment I heard about Edward—I even forgot to switch on the answering machine when I dashed out. Though with things being so quiet, I don't suppose anyone rang.'

Darcy didn't think this was the time to add to her worries by telling her someone had tried to get through. 'They'll ring again if they did,' she consoled.

'Myra stayed in yesterday to take the calls, but she has a heavy date this afternoon.' Myra's heavy dates were numerous, she was one who enjoyed a good time, was Myra, though she never fell down on a job. 'I have to pass the office on my way to the hospital, is it all right with you if I change the tape over to your number?'

'Of course it is.' Darcy didn't stay talking for very long after that. Jane must be out on her feet. She saw she could be more help by getting off the line and letting her try and get some rest. 'Don't think about the office. Between us Myra and I will cope,' she said, and came away from the phone to have Emmy say:

'Come and have something to eat, then you can have a bath and change into some respectable clothes.'

'Yes, Emmy,' said Darcy obediently and over tea and toast was able to relate what Jane had just told her, that there was some improvement in Edward and that he was now out of his coma.

'Will you be going back to the hospital today?' Emmy enquired.

'Jane thinks I'll be more of a help if I stay in and take any telephone calls,' Darcy told her.

But it wasn't until she was in the bath that she had a

chance to review everything that had happened since she had left London on Friday. And by the time her bath was over, feeling more herself wearing her own clothes, Darcy had decided that though at some future date she would have to tell Jane something of what had happened—she had to be warned in case something equally ghastly happened if another delivery job came in, the same fate befalling one of her other temps—that for the moment she would keep quiet. And with Emmy having some bee in her bonnet about going away on holiday, when a holiday hadn't so much as been discussed by them, then rather than have her even more muddled up, she would say nothing of those hours she had been missing to her either. Far better to let her go on thinking she had been at the hospital with Jane the whole time.

But it was during the afternoon, Darcy knowing herself too unsettled to think of studying—not surprising, she thought, that that man Neve should constantly keep popping into her head—that Emmy revealed that her belief she was going on holiday wasn't so confused after all.

'It's four weeks on Saturday that I go,' she said, when somehow or other the seaside town of Brighton had been under discussion for some minutes.

'You're going to Brighton?' Darcy queried, not thinking too much of Emmy's statement, she'd be able to put her right presently.

'Will you be able to manage on your own?' Emmy asked. 'I won't go if you'd rather I didn't, but I did tell Mrs Bricknell to put my name down. By going this early in the year it will be far cheaper than if we left it a while, and we do sometimes have splendid weather in April.'

Darcy let her chat away, but slowly a picture began to emerge. Mrs Bricknell was the chief organiser of the club Emmy belonged to. They must, she concluded, thinking to ring the good lady to find out all the wherefores when she had a chance, have decided last Friday that a week at the seaside would do them all a power of good.

'... and Mrs Bricknell told me I shall need to take my medical card,' Emmy was saying. 'Though I'm feeling so well now I'm sure I shan't need it. And the air's so bracing in Brighton, I'm sure it can do me nothing but good.'

Darcy thought so too. But her intention to ring Mrs Bricknell at the first oppprtunity did not materialise in the week that followed. She didn't want to ring from her home, not that she liked going behind Emmy's back either. But she didn't want her upset that in her caring for her she saw a need to check out some of the things she told her.

And with the office she went to do her clerk-typing stint in on Monday being no bigger than a cubbyhole—she was sure they had never heard of the Act governing office space, or if they had, ignored it—and no telephone available, plus the fact that she was positive they had saved up a mountain of work until she got there, and was kept hard at it, there was no opportunity during the day either.

Lunch hours were used up with a quick sandwich and a race round to the hospital, where she saw Edward, who to everyone's delight was making satisfactory progress, and met Jane for a snatched work-in-hand discussion.

With Edward on the mend, Jane had room to let in her worries about the way the agency was going, and confessed to Darcy that if things didn't pick up soon she would have to think of closing it down.

'Myra told me only yesterday that although she likes the variety, she's not happy not knowing if she's going to be in work from one week to the next,' Jane admitted. 'I've managed to fix her up with something for the next two weeks, but after that . . .'

Jane sighed, with a touch of despair, Darcy saw, privately thinking Myra could have waited a few more days before she told Jane what she had. Edward's accident had been a tremendous upset to her.

'I haven't got a thing for you for next week,' Jane went on, her look of despair deepening.

'Something will turn up,' said Darcy, keeping to herself she was less hopeful than Mr Micawber, 'it always does.'

Jane smiled her thanks. 'That delivery job you did last Friday go off all right?'

'Er—fine.' She would tell her some time, but she hadn't the heart just then.

Darcy went home from work on Friday hoping if that particular firm ever rang through again, then somebody else would get the job. And they probably would ring, she thought, for as it was important that the agency had a good name, she had really put her back into the job.

On phone duty on Sunday while Jane visited the hospital, nothing coming in in the way of work for the next day and the phone staying disquietingly quiet, Darcy was beginning to think that even a job for the firm she had worked for last week would be better than nothing.

By early evening, with still no calls, her sprits were at rock bottom. It did not help that the face of that man Neve intruded so many times, much too often, when by now she should be on the way to putting that nightmare experience behind her. There was a fidgeting in her too which she couldn't put down entirely to her being without a job. Never had she felt so unsettled.

Just after eight the phone rang, giving her spirits a short boost in the hope that some desperate employer had need of the agency's services. Her voice businesslike just in case Jane hadn't got back yet and was now taking the agency calls, Darcy gave her number.

'Relax, it's me,' said Jane, with such a cheerfulness, a lightness in her voice that Darcy just knew something good had happened for her.

'All your Premium Bonds have come up,' she guessed.

'Oh, that I had any! No, it's better than that,' said Jane, still bubbling, going on. 'You've heard of

Macalister Precision Equipment?'

Who hadn't? 'They have branches everywhere, just like the Co-op.'

'Well, guess what,' chortled Jane, and too excited to wait, 'I've just had a phone call—*they* have been *recommended* to *us*!'

'Recommended!' Darcy was stunned, her mind already wondering, who by? Jane was in there again before she could ask.

'Don't you see what this could mean, Darcy?' And, too cock-a-hoop to wait again, although Darcy was beginning to see what it could mean, 'If you do this job well, it could give us an opening into a lot of their business. With the summer holidays coming up . . .'

Darcy just had to stop her. 'Me?' she exclaimed. 'You mean—*I've* got the job?' She was excited too, but at the same time scared. By the sound of it the future of Adaptable Temps could depend on *her*.

'Didn't I say? They asked especially for you.'

'Asked for me?' Darcy gasped, while her mind went in all directions wondering which of the firms she had worked for had recommended her to the mammoth concern. 'Who . . .'

'Who recommended you?' butted in Jane. 'Haven't an idea, but apparently one of the secretaries has gone down with 'flu and thought to phone her boss earlier— he might well have had someone you've done work for dining with him—who cares?' she bubbled. 'The important thing is we've got the job. Isn't it great! Just think, they could pull in another secretary from any one of their dozens of offices, but you've been so highly recommended, they've put the job our way.'

Jane's mood was infectious. And Darcy couldn't help but be thrilled too as she went to tell Emmy she was going to press her best bib and tucker for tomorrow.

'That's nice,' said Emmy placidly when she had finished telling her what it was all about, seeming to think it no more than Darcy's due that she should be so highly recommended. 'I always knew you were the best, dear.' Darcy could do no other than give her a great big hug.

But when she went to bed that night, she would have given anything for Neve whatever-his-name-was to know that far from thinking her the criminal that he did, one of the largest firms in the country had specifically asked that she go and work for them.

The next morning saw her in her best grey light wool mixture suit and on her way to a very important job, undeniable butterflies in her stomach. She had to make a success of this job, she thought, for Jane's sake if not her own; she just had to.

Many times during her journey she reminded herself that her secretarial skills were good. Lord knew she had slogged away hard enough trying to perfect them. But that didn't stop her confidence from giving a rocky shake on its foundations when she found herself outside the imposing entrance of the head office of Macalister Precision Equipment.

She tilted her chin, a confidence there in her stride only she would know was being grabbed at from all quarters, as she went in and up to the enquiry desk where a girl as smart as paint was already on duty.

'My name is Darcy Alexander. I'm from Adaptable Temps,' she said with a smile. 'I believe I'm expected. I . . .'

Before she could get out that she was a replacement secretary for the one who had 'flu, the receptionist was batting her own smile back. She knew already—and there were still a few minutes to go before nine—what it was all about.

'Mr Macalister is expecting you,' she said. And while Darcy was inwardly goggling over that—was she to work for Mr Macalister himself!—the receptionist was busy giving her directions as to where in the vast building she would find Mr Macalister.

Darcy tried to quell the anxiety making itself felt in her insides as she rode upwards in the lift. It couldn't be *the* Mr Macalister, she reasoned. Macalister wasn't such a common name, admittedly, but in an outfit this size, there just had to be more than one.

Stepping out of the lift, she counted down the doors in the corridor until she was sure she had the right one. Though when she saw a girl coming by, she thought to make absolutely certain.

'Excuse me, is this Mr Macalister's office?' she asked.

'Yes, through there,' the girl answered, eyeing her with some curiosity. 'Have you an appointment?' And smiling, she confided warningly, 'Mr Macalister's a workoholic—nobody ever breaks into his work load without an appointment.'

It looked very much as though her nose was going to be kept very firmly to the grindstone again this week, but Darcy smiled back. Hard work had never bothered her.

'He's expecting me,' she said, and opened the door.

The office she found herslf in was empty, but there was another door leading off it. Mr Macalister's office, no doubt, she thought. And hoping he wasn't going to bite her head off at the first interruption in his workoholic work load day, she paused for a moment to recharge her confidence. Then since there was no way she could start work without interrupting him, she went forward. Outside the closed door, she paused briefly to take a deep breath, then setting a smile on her face, she knocked firmly and went in.

The first thing she saw was a large solid-looking desk. The next, in that split second of entering, was a hand— a hand holding a gold pen that looked so startlingly familiar, all her nerve ends jangled as her eyes flew upwards to the face of the dark-suited man who sat behind the desk.

Shock like that of unexpectedly hitting a brick wall vibrated her being. A pair of piercing flint-hard eyes looked back at her. Piercing eyes she would never ever forget. Eyes that had been with her many, many times this last seven days. And so great was her shock, her vocal cords just refused to function.

Not so the man who sat watching her every reaction. The smile he gave—hers had long since gone to ground—had nothing pleasant about it the moment before his smile too was discarded, and he said:

'Good morning, Darcy. Your reprehensible driving got you home without mishap, I trust?'

CHAPTER SIX

'You!'

So shaken was Darcy to see Neve calmly sitting there, his expression as hard and uncompromising as ever she had seen it, that for one crazy world-spinning moment she thought she was going to faint. Not that he would help her to a chair this time, or go for a glass of water, she thought, as her world righted itself. She had considered all the trauma that had arisen from that delivery job was over. But in that first look at him, she knew that it wasn't.

'You're—Mr Macalister?' she asked chokily, not needing that brief inclination of his head for confirmation.

Without needing to think about it, swiftly she turned. He'd punished her once for something she had no knowledge of, she wasn't going to put her head on the chopping block a second time.

She had made it to the outer door when his voice stopped her from going through it. And then all her instincts of self-preservation urged her to ignore his drawled, 'Mrs Davis is going to be delighted when she hears how you walked out on your assignment without so much as staying to take the cover from the typewriter.'

Darcy froze, but would not turn around. She stayed where she was, made to by her loyalty to Jane—that loyalty in conflict with what every screaming nerve was telling her to do.

'When I spoke with her yesterday she sounded as though work coming her way from Macalisters was the realisation of all her hopes and dreams,' Neve Macalister advised mockingly.

She did turn then, and there was hate in her eyes.

Hate that she had to go against what she wanted to do. Hate that because of Jane she couldn't tell him to go to hell and take his job with him.

'You spoke to Jane?' she questioned, not yet ready to believe what her brain was telling her, that this was Macalister, the boss man himself. 'Are you the personnel manager?'

An insincere smile lifted one corner of his mouth. 'Apart from my brother, there's only one other Macalister in the building,' he said sardonically.

Darcy remembered Blair—would she ever forget the way he had come upon her and this . . . She concentrated on trying to bring Blair's face to mind. He had looked to be about twenty-five. He had a good-humoured face she remembered, and looked to be a pleasant young man. But there had been none of the authority about him that there was about Neve, and she didn't need to go any further to know which of the two brothers ran Macalister Precision Equipment. Neve Macalister was the big chief. There was no one higher she could appeal to, no one to whom she could plead a clash of personalities.

And she knew then that if she walked out as she wanted to, Adaptable Temps would be finished with Macalisters—and with the pull he undoubtedly had; a word here and there in the right direction, and Adaptable Temps would find it difficult to get any worthwhile work anywhere else.

Hating him as she had never hated anyone in her whole life, she walked slowly back into his office. Hate showing in her eyes as her face sternly controlled, she looked at him.

'*You swine!*' she hissed through clenched teeth and hated him the more that he was entirely unmoved by her hate.

'Staying?' he queried laconically.

Darcy threw him a searing look, then marched back into the other room. The temper in her was barely constrained as she went to the desk and yanked the cover from the typewriter it housed.

Workoholic was not the name for it, she thought by the time midday arrived—and she had thought she had worked hard last week! The man was a maniac for work, not sparing himself, not sparing her either. She recalled her introduction to him, that moment when she had opened her eyes in his study. Almost the first thing she had seen was him at work—and that had been at *four in the morning*—did the man never stop?

At one o'clock Darcy ceased typing. He had commanded her to leave the door open when she had exited from his dictation, but she knew it wasn't because in his rare moments of raising his eyes he liked the look of her. It gave him satisfaction to have her there against her inclination. She was hating the situation—he was enjoying it immensely. Her calling him a swine was an insult to the whole pig family.

The non-sound of her typewriter broke into his concentration, and, as she had hoped, not wanting to go into his office unless ordered—he never requested—he looked up.

'Do I get a lunch hour?' she asked bluntly, no smile about her; though she did thinks he might smile on the day his secretary returned.

'Be back at two sharp,' he grunted, and would have buried his head in his work again, only Darcy got in there quickly with a sarcastic:

'I'll run all the way.'

He needn't think just because he was calling the shots that she was going to sit there and take all he threw like some timid dormouse, she thought, as she sat in a park eating a sandwich. Though it hadn't pleased her to see what had looked like the merest twitch of his lips, as though her snappy exit comeback had amused him.

She hadn't amused him, she concluded. He'd probably had some acid remark ready to fling back at her, but had decided he would rather get on with his work than bandy words with her.

At five to two she re-entered the Macalister building,

already looking forward to five o'clock when she could go home to dear Emmy whose sweet nature would be a welcome relief. Damn, she had forgotten to ring Mrs Bricknell about that holiday. Well, she wasn't going to ring from the office—she didn't want *him* knowing anything of her private life.

His head was still bent over his work when she went in. She wondered if he had been out for lunch. Surely he couldn't go a full day working the way he did without stoking up! Why the heck should she care anyway? Darcy got on with her typing.

Just before three Neve Macalister put down his pen and strolled into her office. Darcy carried on typing. If he wanted to say anything to her, the floor was his.

He had nothing to say, apparently which caused her to wonder if it was a habit of his to prowl around his secretary's office every afternoon at three.

His presence unnerved her. She didn't want it to, as she carried on tapping away, but it did. If he wanted a rest, why didn't he go and rest in his own room? she thought, her annoyance with herself that she let him unnerve her transferring to him.

He had been in her office two or three minutes when the thought came that he was either getting ready to pounce or—or he must be waiting for something. She made a mistake, and it was all his fault. The typewriter was the latest kind with a lift-off tape that quickly pulled off wrong characters. Darcy back spaced to her error, still wondering what it was he was waiting for. Was tea usually brought in around this time? Was he expecting her to go and get it?

The sound of the door opening had her thinking the tea must have arrived, and her eyes went to him expecting to see his eyes on the door. But they were not on the door. He wasn't watching the door. He was watching *her*!

Puzzlement was with her, the question rearing—why? Her glance slithered off him as a female voice made itself heard, a familiarity there that had her knowing it wasn't the tea lady.

'Really, Neve, I was up to my eyes in committee work! What's so essential that I had to come and see you straight away?'

Darcy looked at the blonde woman, who apparently didn't waste her time noticing secretaries, and any notion she had received that Neve Macalister had been watching her with some purpose went straight out of her head.

For she knew the woman, although of course the woman didn't know her. But she had seen her often enough on television, and recognised her as Cordelia Cunliffe, a woman who was forever airing her views on this, that and the other.

'I wouldn't have phoned had it not been important,' she heard Neve reply.

And while Darcy's eyes were starting to goggle that Cordelia Cunliffe had gone over to Neve Macalister and laid a fond hand on his arm—it occurred to her that they knew each other in more than a casual way—she heard her exclaiming urgently, either dismissing her sitting there as beneath her notice; or, by the sound of it, her panic making her forget there was another pair of ears present.

'Neve! It has nothing to do with Gus Stoddart, has it? I thought you'd dealt with that for me—you said you had. I...'

Darcy was left staring after them. For, not giving her time to say more, though Darcy had heard enough to give her plenty to think about, Neve had thrown one darkly suspicious glance her way, and then hurried the other woman into his office, and closed the door.

They were closeted together for about half an hour, ample time for Darcy, her mind still boggling, to sort out that the holier-than-thou Cordelia Cunnliffe—wife of James Cunliffe, eminent surgeon, though not so lofty with his views as his wife—must be having an affair with none other than Mr—bear with a sore head would be sweeter—Neve Macalister!

Now wasn't *that* a turn-up! Darcy remembered seeing Cordelia Cunliffe on television only a couple of weeks ago. The press had got hold of some story about her husband refusing to perform an abortion on some woman in desperate circumstances, and she had been giving vigorous support to her husband's stand against abortion.

But it was the interview she had given some time before that that Darcy was recalling. It had been about the time some divorce statistics had been announced. Cordelia Cunliffe had really got on her soapbox then, declaring that marriage should be a lifetime commitment. Though it was what Darcy remembered her saying after that that she found mind blowing. She was sure, positive, that she had trotted out something to the effect that in her view, once married, one should stay faithful to one's partner for life!

Oh, wouldn't the press have a heyday if they got to hear just how faithful the not so wifely blonde was being!

Into her head shot the memory of the blonde who had driven away from Neve's home in Cornthorpe, and added to that the fear in Cordelia's voice when she'd said, 'It has nothing to do with Gus Stoddart, has it?' Darcy had good cause to remember the name Stoddart and saw then the reason why Cordelia Cunliffe had sounded panicky. If Stoddart had got hold of a love-letter between Neve and Cordelia, then she would be panic-stricken, wouldn't she? By the look of it, she wanted Neve *and* her marriage. How about that for being faithful for life!

Having sorted out just what was going on between the two in there, Darcy knew puzzlement that with Neve suspecting she hadn't known the name of the woman he was having an affair with—that much had been made plain when he'd asked if she had recognised her that day he had frightened her so much she'd nearly tried her hand at flying. Why then, still believing her capable of blackmail, had he insisted that his mistress come to the office at a time when he knew she would be there? When he knew she wasn't so dim that she couldn't put two and two together? Surely it would have occurred to him, not trusting her, that once she had the lady's name she would be in a position to blab it to the newspapers.

And why, she wondered, even more puzzled, had he specifically asked for her when his secretary had succumbed to 'flu. He'd guessed at her loyalty to Jane, of course—it must have been about her when she had told him how desperate they were for work—proved in the fact she was still here and hadn't marched out of the office at two minutes past nine this morning. She had reasoned shortly after that to have her hating to be there was just one more delightful instance of him making her pay for something she hadn't done. But was it?

She gave it up. She couldn't make sense of any of it. None of it made sense. Neither, she thought, trying to direct her thoughts into other channels, did it make sense that she should feel hurt to know that whatever his reasons, Neve Macalister didn't trust her.

Darcy had got over the ridiculous notion that she felt anything at all that her temporary boss didn't trust her by the time the door opened and he escorted his departing guest through her office. She didn't care a button what he thought, she determined.

'It's about time you came and had dinner with James and me,' she heard Cordelia say on her way out.

Talk about two-faced! Darcy thought, as the door closed and Neve Macalister came and stood over her, the muttered, 'Charming!' that left her not lost on him, even if he made her repeat it.

'What did you say?' he asked grimly.

A coward's streak touched her so that for a brief instant she refused to repeat it. Then anger started to burn inside. Just who did he think he was? Just who did Cordelia Cunliffe think she was, spouting the odds on being for ever faithful? The pair of them wanted locking up?

'I said, charming,' she said defiantly.

'Meaning?' he questioned grittily, everything about him saying she was at the bottom of his popularity poll.

'How you can contemplate having dinner at the table of your mistress's husband's home defeats me,' she said disgustedly. 'It's . . .'

'Mistress!'

She threw him a look that should have shrivelled him, but didn't. 'You haven't that much honour, have you?' she flared, not knowing why she was growing so angry; it was nothing at all to do with her what any of the despotic trio got up to. 'You don't even have the honour to admit that Cordelia Cunliffe is your . . .'

Hands she had forgotten could be so hard clamped ruthlessly down on her shoulders as he fairly lifted her out of her chair to stand in front of him.

'Don't talk to me about honour,' he snarled. 'You think the game you were engaged in before I put a stop to it was honourable?'

Darcy knew she would be wasting her time in trying to vindicate herself. But the longer she was taking to reply, the more agonising his grip on her shoulders was becoming, but some stubbornness in her made her determined not to show it.

'I wonder you didn't arrange to meet her somewhere else,' she taunted. 'If I'm such an out-and-out criminal, what's to stop me from watching points and trying my hand again?'

It was the wrong thing to have said. She knew that from the flame in his eyes. She saw she had only succeeded in infuriating him more—saw that, even before she heard the words roar in her ears:

'You *admit* it?'

'No—No,' she said hurriedly, and on a cry of pain she was unable to keep in as his grip intensified, she found she was moaning, 'You're hurting me, Neve!'

'I'd like to . . .' he began to thunder. Then he saw the shimmer of tears in her eyes. She saw the white line of fury round his mouth disappear as his eyes went to his hands, to where he was brutally holding her. Then what he would 'like to' was never heard.

And, so suddenly, she hadn't an idea what he was about, he had those same hands beneath her shirt, beneath her lacy bra straps; his eyes catching the same glimpse she did, as she turned her head, of her reddened skin.

'I didn't mean to ...' he muttered, as in soothing movements his hands stroked backwards and forwards over her burning shoulders, again not finishing the sentence he had begun.

And if Darcy thought he had been on the way to apologising, then that thought soon went hurtling out of her head. For the shock of having his hands inside her shirt, the shock of actually discovering—now that those hands were being caressing as opposed to what she had felt was the near pulverisation of her bones— that she didn't find his hands on her anywhere near as distasteful as she should, was staggering.

But it was when his touch, still soothing her bruised skin, still caressing, started to make the oddest of sensations felt in her, unbelievable when she hated him so, that it came to her that this had gone on for long, long enough.

Abruptly she jerked away and tried hard to speak coldly as she rounded on him. 'When I fancy being mauled around, Mr Macalister,' she said, chagrined to discover her voice was husky, not cold the way she wanted, 'then,' she made herself continue, 'permit me to tell you that you'll be the *last* to know!'

Steadily Neve looked at her flushed face, the narrowing of his eyes telling her her remark was going to come bouncing back with a bonus. She didn't have to wait very long for it.

'I believe I once told you, Miss Alexander,' he replied, the evenness of his words telling her he was keeping his temper in check, 'that the idea of being the first with you held no appeal. Permit me to rephrase that. I would be relieved if you could make that—never.' And before she had swallowed that, he was firing, 'Isn't it time you got on with the work I'm paying you to do?'

On the stroke of five Darcy packed up and went home. After his insufferable parting shot—she would have been hard at it if he hadn't made a grab for her and yanked her out of her chair—Neve Macalister had not spoken another word to her. She didn't feel like calling out goodnight.

Emmy was eager to hear all about her day when she arrived home. And rather than have her worried on her behalf, Darcy told her nothing about the vile creature it was her misfortune to work for—with luck his secretary would make a speedy recovery in the next few days.

But it was over their meal that Emmy pressed for more than that it was a pleasant office, had modern office equipment, and that the work was interesting. 'But what's Mr Macalister like?' she asked, and really wanted to know.

'He's—a tall man.'

'Over six feet?' Darcy nodded, and Emmy smiled. 'Is he married?'

'No.' Emmy invariably asked that question. 'Though I'm certain he has a lot of girl-friends.' And one in particular, but it would be too involved, as well as worrying for Emmy, if she got stuck into that.

'None as pretty as you, I'll bet,' said Emmy out of the love she had for her. 'Is he a nice man, though?'

Darcy bit back the truth. She hated lying to her, but if Emmy suspected every day until his secretary came back was going to be purgatory for her, she would only get upset.

'He's super,' she said, and was glad she had when Emmy sighed contentedly and turned on to another subject.

She was glad Emmy could not see her 'super' boss the next day. Morose wasn't the word for him. Darcy went home that night wondering how she was ever going to pretend he was the last word in kindly bosses to Emmy. If he'd had a mouthful of gumboils he couldn't have been more monosyllabic than he had been that day.

Even her dictation had been put on tape so he didn't have to bother himself with talking to her.

And that was all right with her. The least contact she had with him the better as far as she was concerned. Though she had been aware he was watching her.

Wednesday was a repeat of Tuesday, with Darcy well aware of the distrustful looks that came her way in hard-eyed darts from time to time. She tried to ignore Neve Macalister, but when she returned from lunch, she had to admit he was wearing her down.

It was a relief when she returned to her desk, threw the briefest of glances into the other room while she stowed her bag, to see, when she did a quick double take, that Neve wasn't there.

Hoping that wherever he was it kept him busy until after five, she got stuck into her work. Whatever happened she wasn't going to let the agency down. It was only the thought of Jane that had her returning after lunch anyway.

She was solidly at work when two hours later the door opened. Well, if he thought she was going to look up and wish him good afternoon he had another think coming! She heard him move, knew he was to the side of her, but kept her head bent.

That was until, from the corner of her eye, she saw the dark figure stoop just as though he was bending to see into her face. And then she looked at him. Only it wasn't him, it was his brother.

Blair straightened up as she sat back, a natural curve to his mouth as he cracked, 'I thought it was you—though you had a shade more colour in your face the last time I saw you.'

Pink coloured her face again as she recalled the moment; she had been lying on the bed, Neve over her. Lost for something very brilliant to say, Darcy advised, 'Mr Macalister is out. He didn't say when he . . .'

'Mr Macalister, eh?' Blair grinned. And, tongue in cheek, 'I sort of got the impression you were more friendly than that with Neve.'

It became obvious to her then, with Blair grinning
like a Cheshire cat, his manner markedly different from
that of his brother, that he couldn't know anything of
the reason she had been in his brother's home that
weekend, that he knew nothing of the blackmail
attempt. Perhaps he didn't even know Cordelia Cunliffe
was his brother's latest girl-friend.

She was sure of it when she heard his next remark. For
it was clear Blair thought *she* was Neve Macalister's
latest.

'It's not like Neve to mix business with pleasure,' he
said, his look speculative, and that easy grin widening.
'Would this be a sign—since he obviously can't see
enough of you—that my dear brother is going to take
the plunge?'

Her eyes widened at the very thought of her ever
being married to such a man as Neve Macalister, and
she lost no time in steamrollering Blair's specula-
tions.

'Your brother is *not* mixing business with pleasure,'
she told him with a fair degree of frost. 'My—er—rela-
tionship with N——Mr Macalister ended that day—
er—that weekend I was at his home.'

'It doesn't look like it from where I'm seeing it,' said
Blair incorrigibly. And, with that wide smile again, 'It's
got to be serious if Neve had you stay at home for a
weekend.' And when he saw the way she bit her lip at
her slip in letting him know that much, he teased, 'Did
you forget to tell him it's all over?' Going on when she
decided it was best not to answer, 'Though come to
think of it, you'd be the first woman ever to do so.' And
at her wide-eyed stare, 'It's always been Neve's pre-
rogative to end . . .'

'There was nothing to end,' Darcy jumped in, thinking
it was about time she did something about concluding
this conversation. Then she saw Blair was remembering
what he had seen, and coloured. 'Well, it's all over now,'
she added lamely.

'But Neve isn't believing it.' There was still that

speculative look about him. It told her he remained unconvinced.

'Look,' she said, finding him almost as exasperating as she found his brother. 'Ne . . .' Oh, what the dickens did it matter what she called him? 'Neve's secretary happens to have gone down with 'flu. I work for a temps agency, so when he rang Mrs Davis who runs the agency . . .'

'He rang personally?' Blair picked her up. 'He didn't happen to ask for you by name, did he?'

There was nothing wrong with his intelligence, Darcy saw. She could argue with him until she was blue in the face, but he would still go on thinking exactly what he wanted to think. She refused to smile as his engaging grin came out again, and was just about to tell him she would pass any message on to Neve when he came in— hoping Blair wouldn't want a bigger hint than that to get him to leave—when he suddenly said, his tone serious:

'Don't give Neve a hard time, there's a love.' And while she was wishing it in her power to do just that, he went on, still assuming she knew his brother far better than she did—with some justification from the evidence he had, she realised, 'He's probably told you how our parents died when my sister and I were small. What he hasn't told you, if I know Neve, is how he slaved to get the company on its feet. He laboured night and day to get things going, so that in the end work became like a drug to him.'

'He still found time to play, I gather,' Darcy said caustically, a picture of Cordelia Cunliffe's hand, familiar on his arm, stirring acid in her, swamping the finer feeling she had that she should be stopping him from giving her this personal insight into the hard man she knew. Then she very nearly dropped when Blair answered:

'Don't be jealous of past affairs,' too clearly mis-interpreting her acid. 'Neve had some fun due to him. He was both mother and father to Cordelia and me after our parents died . . .'

What else he said after that was lost to Darcy as her
mind stuck fast on the name Cordelia that had floated
in the air. Cordelia! she thought, reeling. Was he saying
that Cordelia Cunliffe was his sister? Neve's sister too?
Not his mistress, as she had jumped in with both feet
and assumed!

Apparently he was. She came out from the stupefaction of her thoughts to hear Blair Macalister asking,
entirely unaware that he had said anything out of the
ordinary, 'Have you met my sister Cordelia yet?'

'Er—briefly,' Darcy replied, and gathering her wits
together. 'I've seen her on television, of course, often.'

Blair grinned at that 'often', then remarked, 'For all
Cordelia's good works, Neve has always refused to
become one of them.'

'Oh?' Strangely, she found herself wanting to hear
more, the words just not coming to tell him he was
wrong to give her these family confidences.

'She's been badgering at him for years now, telling
him it was about time he eased up and took a wife. But
he's always said marriage wasn't for him. Reckoned he'd
seen too many broken marriages to want marriage for
himself.'

It was then her latent sense of the rightness of what
he was telling her gave Darcy a nudge. 'Look, Blair,'
she tried, about to stop him from revealing anything
else. But she didn't get the chance.

'You know *my* name, even though we never did get
formally introduced,' he butted in, a wicked look danc-
ing in his eyes.

She took the hint. 'Darcy Alexander,' she said, and
saw that wicked look fade as he took her right hand in
what might have been a formal handshake. Only it was
more friendly than that, as solemnly he said:

'Be kind to my brother, Darcy Alexander. He doesn't
wear his heart on his sleeve, and he can be a bear sometimes I know. But he must care for you, or he would
have got any one of the secretaries here to fill in.'

'He . . .' was as far as her protest got.

'And you, despite what you're not saying, must feel something for him too,' he went on, 'or why else are you here? You could have refused, and if as you've said it's all over between you, he would have understood.'

'Blair, I . . .'

And it seemed then that between one brother and the other, she was never going to finish a sentence, for just at that moment, with Blair still holding on to her hand, the door opened, and in walked Neve Macalister.

Blair seemed in no hurry to let go her hand—had probably forgotten he still had hold of it, she thought, looking from him to his grim-faced brother. Neve's hard-eyed look boded ill, she saw, as stern-faced he observed that valuable time was being wasted while they dallied holding hands.

'Haven't you got any work to do?' he fired at the pair of them.

Without haste, Blair let go her hand, a smile curving his mouth. 'There's a little green-eyed monster to the north of Katmandu,' he misquoted outrageously, making Darcy want to hide under the table at his inference that Neve's attitude stemmed from his being jealous on coming in and finding them holding hands.

'What are you doing here, Blair?' Clearly Neve Macalister was in no mood for his brother's banter.

'Well, I was on the point of asking Darcy for a date,' said Blair unblinking, when Darcy knew full well he had no such intention. 'If you have no objection, that is?'

Darcy's colour was a furious red when Blair strolled out and Neve slammed into his office. She knew full well from Blair's huge grin that the harsh reply he received had been all the confirmation he needed that his brother was serious about her. He thought the signal sent his way was a 'hands off, she's mine' signal. But she had interpreted differently the angry, 'I have every objection,' Neve had flung at him. She knew it meant only one thing. Neve Macalister wasn't having the brother he had been guardian to getting snared up with the likes of her. And that made her angry—too angry then to think of analysing any of what Blair had told her.

Emmy again asked after her temporary boss when Darcy got home, beaming contentedly, all happy with her world, blissfully unaware of the hard work her young companion found it to continue the myth that her boss was 'super'.

And because Emmy was in a talkative mood that night, it was not until Darcy went to bed that it came to her to unravel any of what had been said that afternoon.

She still felt wounded from Neve Macalister's 'I have every objection', even though she didn't understand why anything he said should possibly wound her. Why should she care? There was no answer.

It was obvious Blair thought Neve *was* mixing business with pleasure, she thought sourly. Well, just let him wait around, he would soon see that there would be no ding-dong of wedding bells for his brother—not with her as his bride anyway.

Sleepless as she lay in bed, she decided not to think about Neve Macalister. She would only get angry, and that wasn't conducive to sleep. And she felt wide awake now, without any interference from him.

She recalled the shock she had received on learning that Cordelia Cunliffe was not his mistress but his sister. Ought she to apologise? And on the heels of that thought—why should she? He'd jumped to conclusions about her and never looked like apologising. Okay, so he had some justification, but ... Oh, damn him!

Darcy thought she had succeeded in shutting the whole Macalister family out of her mind, thought she was on the way to drifting into sleep. Then suddenly a thought hit her that was so sharp it had her opening her eyes and sitting bolt upright in her bed.

She had thought it was Neve Macalister who was being threatened with blackmail. But it couldn't be! For in recalling the panic that had been in Cordelia's voice, Darcy also remembered her fevered, 'I thought you'd dealt with that,' in the office on Monday. And in re-

membering, Darcy knew positively that it was not Neve
Gus Stoddart had threatened, but Cordelia. For
Cordelia had added two words to that 'I thought you'd
dealt with that', and positive she was right, Darcy
recalled that those two words were, 'for me'!

Neve Macalister was in a foul mood the next day,
though it was a wonder to Darcy how she recognised it
as any different from his mood all week, because the
milk of human kindness had not been exactly flowing
freely on the previous three days.

But foul mood it was, the looks he spared her blacker
than ever, his orders barked at her shortly, concisely,
his brow coming down if she didn't understand him
straight away.

And it had touched her mind to *apologise* to him! she
fumed, storming out of his office after being rounded
on for taking him in a wrong file. She must have been
touched to let the thought of apologising visit her even
briefly! How was she supposed to know, with two files
labelled identically, that one was incoming the other
outgoing? He, of course, had wanted the other one.

On Friday she had had enough. Surely his secretary
would be fit for work on Monday. And if she wasn't,
well then, Myra could jolly well come in and take over—
he'd get no change out of Myra.

Darcy sighed near to despair as she recalled Jane telling her that Myra, at a time when Jane could do without added worry, had told her she was thinking of leaving, and knew then that if the 'flu-stricken secretary
wasn't fit by Monday, then she would have to return. It
was stretching her loyalty to Jane, but Myra's loyalty
wouldn't stand up at all if Neve Macalister barked at
Myra the way he had barked at her. Myra would walk
out—the chance of Adaptable Temps being called on
again walking out with her.

Besides which, she thought, picking up the phone
automatically when it rang, it wasn't Myra he had asked
for, it was her—a substitute just wouldn't be acceptable.
Stifling a second sigh, she spoke efficiently into the

phone. And it was just as though her thoughts had conjured her up, because she heard the voice on the other end introducing herself as Avril Knight, Mr Macalister's secretary, who then went on to say she had rung to see if there were any queries she could help with.

Delighted to hear her sounding so well, not so much as a trace of a cold in her voice, let alone 'flu, Darcy answered, 'I don't think so,' her spirits already lifting to hear the other girl sounding so well. 'How are you?'

'Fine, just fine,' Avril Knight replied, sending her spirits soaring. 'And you?'

'Shan't be sorry when this week is over,' said Darcy, not giving a damn that Neve Macalister raised his head at that moment and glowered at her. And, fingers crossed, 'You'll be in on Monday?'

'Well—er—— Did Mr Macalister say he was expecting me back?' she asked hesitatingly, without knowing it, sending Darcy's mercury sky-high. 'When he rang me last Sunday he said I'd looked tired. Even apologised for working me so hard, but told me not to worry about the office, that he would contact me when to come back.'

The swine! The perfect swine! His secretary hadn't had 'flu at all! Quietly seething, Darcy managed, 'I can understand that.' And looking straight into his eyes through the open door way, her own eyes glinting, 'But if you feel up to it, could you come in on Monday? Mr Macalister was going to give you a ring . . .'

She heard the smile in the other girl's voice. 'Only he's got his head down. Rather pipped him at the post by calling in, didn't I?' she added, as if it was a first.

Having got Avril Knight's confirmation that she would be there on Monday, Darcy replaced the phone and got to her feet. She met Neve coming from his office, his expression, to put it mildly, not very promising.

Sweetly, Darcy got in first. 'Miss Knight has fully recovered from her *illness*, and will report on Monday.'

'When I want you to run this office I'll say so,' he replied curtly.

There was no sign of sweetness in the air, phoney or otherwise, as almost toe to toe they stood and glared at each other.

'Then you shouldn't go around telling lies,' she snapped.

'What I did was relatively innocent compared with your criminal intent,' was her short answer.

'I did not attempt to blackmail you!' Darcy said hotly, her voice near to yelling in her frustration at not being able to get it through his thick skull that she had merely been a pawn in the filthy scheming of Stoddart. And remembering, 'Though it wasn't you who was being threatened, was it—it was your sister.'

Too late she saw that what she had just said must seem like the reverse of a denial of guilt, her guilt proven with her knowing it was Cordelia who was being black-mailed. She winced as hard hands gripped her shoulders, Neve's angry look telling her she'd be lucky if all he did was shake her.

'What's the matter?'

His question was unexpected. Then she realised he must have seen her wince. But even so, his question was still unexpected. And no reason at all, she thought, to keep from him what a brute he had been.

'I'm still wearing the bruises from the last time you had a go at cracking my bones,' she told him pugnaci-ously, and was surprised then to feel the sudden relief from pain as he too remembered the redness his hands had left behind on her shoulders.

But even with his hands now away from her, Darcy saw there was still a mighty aggression in him. She had no intention of staying quiet waiting for it to go out of control again.

'I didn't even know Mrs Cunliffe was your sister until the other day when Blair told me. If you remember, I thought ...' She stopped. If she went on like this the next thing she knew she would be apologising to him.

'From what I overheard her say on Monday I was able to work out for myself that . . .' His eyes glinted, and it was then that Darcy came near to exploding. 'I *do* have a normal supply of intelligence, you know,' she said heatedly. 'It was obvious when I remembered what she said—I don't have to be in league with Stoddart to work out . . .' She stopped again, another idea popping into her head. And as the idea stuck, so her eyes grew large. 'She was having an affair with him, wasn't she!' she gasped.

Then she had cause to back hurriedly away when his hands came from where they were safely down at his sides. 'Did Stoddart tell you that?' he asked, coming after her.

'No, he didn't,' she shouted. 'And—and keep your hands to yourself!'

She saw those hands clench, knew then that he loved his family so much he would do anything to protect them. She thought of Emmy and how she would do the same. But there was something in her that just refused to let her back down.

'The letter all the fuss is about is one your sister wrote to Stoddart, isn't it?'

She wished she hadn't, wished she had kept quiet. For there was no way she was going to make it to the door before Neve caught her. And he looked ready to pulversise the whole of her, not just her shoulders.

And then, when she thought she'd be lucky to complete one full week working for him, he stopped.

'Mind your own bloody business!'

And with that, as though needing to be where she was not in order to gain some of his lost control, he strode past her and out into the corridor.

Darcy returned to her seat, but saw her fingers were shaking too much for her to contemplate typing.

The hours went by until five o'clock without her seeing him again. But by the time that hour was reached, she had begun to wonder, with his parting remark of, 'Mind your own bloody business!' if that could mean he might be beginning to believe she had nothing to do with that other business either!

Was she crazy to think that? He hadn't let Cordelia down by admitting that his sister had written some compromising letter to Stoddart, but by not letting her know, wasn't he admitting that family loyalty said no one else should know? That if she didn't know—a doubt there about her guilt—then he couldn't be the one to tell her.

She didn't like Neve Macalister. She hated him most of the time. Yet she couldn't help smiling softly, that maybe he was beginning to see he had been totally wrong about her. She stood up, dropping the cover over the typewriter ready for Avril Knight on Monday. What did it matter anyway what he thought? she pondered. She wouldn't be seeing him again, would she? Her smile disappeared.

CHAPTER SEVEN

HAVING finished her temporary employment with Macalister Precision Equipment on Friday, Darcy admitted in the weekend that followed that she was spending far too much time in thinking about Neve Macalister.

It was natural she should rail against him, she told herself. He had made her cross, livid, wasn't understating it. But, that being so, why then did she not only remember the times he had looked ready to set about her, but also have her anger against him tempered with memories of the times he had been gentle with her?

Jane ringing her on Saturday afternoon was a welcome interruption from incessant thoughts of him. 'How did it go at Macalister's?' she asked, and Darcy smothered a sigh. And she had thought to forget him for a while!

'Fine,' she lied. And mainly for Jane's sake, though truthfully, 'He had no complaints about my work.' Then she heard Jane go very nearly ecstatic when she heard who 'he' was.

'You mean you worked for Mr Macalister himself!' she squeaked.

'He's quite human when you get to know him.' Darcy was back to telling lies again. And, not liking the way this conversation was centring on Neve Macalister, she got in there quickly to ask how Edward was.

'He's picked up so much this week,' Jane replied happily. 'With luck I shall soon have him home.'

They chatted on some more, mostly about Edward. Jane then went on to tell Darcy she had another secretarial job for her on Monday, and heard from Darcy that Emmy was well, and that there were no restrictions that prevented her taking the job.

'Good,' she said, then launched into the details Darcy
needed to know for Monday.

On Sunday, much as Darcy tried to rid her mind of
Neve, he was there in her mind on waking. Again she
told herself it was natural. Wouldn't any girl be the
same? What girl would stand being accused as she had
been accused and not have it niggle away at her? She
had thought on Friday afternoon that he had come a
little way from his suspicions of her, but on thinking
about it, she knew he hadn't.

Avril Knight revealing that she had been deliberately
got out of the way so that he could have her under his
eye niggled at her too. She saw why, of course. He had
wanted her there where he could see her if and when
Stoddart, recovered from his beating, had the nerve to
once again try to blackmail his sister. Lord knew how
long Neve would have had her working in his office if
Avril, dutiful secretary that she was, hadn't thought to
telephone in.

On Monday, her best foot forward, Darcy went along
to her new temporary employer—and discovered that
compared to the work she had done last week, the
week's secretarial job was dull, dull, dull.

She was glad when Friday arrived, and went home
that night wondering if all future secretarial jobs were
going to be the same. Not once this week had she found
anything stimulating in the work she did. Not like last
week when, though admittedly it had been a hard slog,
there had been a breath of life, stimulus in most of the
things she had done.

Emmy came out of her bedroom as Darcy went in.
'Had a good day, dear?' she enquired.

'Not sorry to have finished this particular job, Emmy,'
Darcy told her, and saw the old lady smile, as she
replied:

'Not all men are as super as Mr Macalister, are they?'
And, not waiting for an answer, 'I thought we'd have
dinner early tonight.'

Darcy had no objection, and didn't think to question why particularly they should have dinner early that night. If Emmy wanted dinner early, it was all right by her.

But once the dinner dishes were washed and Emmy remarked, 'I'm rather busy,' and straightaway trotted along to her bedroom, it came to Darcy that she had better go after her and see what she was busy at. She restrained the impulse, getting out her exercise books instead. Emmy was entitled to her privacy. No doubt she would tell her all about it in due time.

When an hour later Emmy still hadn't come from her room, Darcy began to grow anxious. Several times she had wanted to go and see what the old lady was doing. Perhaps she could help her? She closed her exercise books; nothing was going in anyway. Then knowing it wasn't just curiosity, she got to her feet to go and see if Emmy was all right.

The phone rang before she got as far as the sitting room door. She remembered she was on call that night, as Jane had a dinner engagement, one she hadn't been able to get out of, with little Edward's paternal grandparents.

She picked up the phone and gave her number. Then she clutched on to the phone, momentarily speechless as she heard Neve Macalister's firm authoritative voice.

Her first thought was to wonder if he had phoned her direct or if he had phoned the agency first. She had the answer in his cool clipped words, and knew then she would wait for ever if she was expecting him to apologise for the vile things he thought of her.

'I need you for the weekend,' he said without preamble, having recognised her voice and sounding, despite the fact that it was he who had made the call, not too pleased to hear it.

Darcy knew it was business, but her acid was charged that he wasn't sounding to be very pleasant about it.

'Does Miss Knight have 'flu?' she queried sweetly. That girl she had met in the corridor was right when she

said he was a workoholic. What other head of company
went to his office on Saturday *and* Sunday?

'She happens to be Mrs Knight. Her place is with her
husband at the weekend, not in my home.'

She didn't want to work for him again. Perhaps Myra
. . . His home! Her thoughts came to an abrupt stand-
still. Had he said . . .

'Your home!' she choked. 'You want me to work in
your home?'

'Tomorrow and Sunday. You'll have to stay overnight.' His tone brooked no refusal.

'I can't,' she said without having to think about it—
and had his reply in her ear in double quick time.

'Why can't you?' he rapped. Then he was hitting her
with, 'You're going away with some man for the weekend,' and the name cracking like a whiplash, 'Stoddart!'

Where before she had been ready to scream at him
that she didn't know Stoddart, this time there was
nothing but weary frustration in her. Quietly, she told
him, 'There is no man. I have no plans to go away anywhere.'

To which he came back promptly, 'So you're available
to come to me on Saturday.'

Even if there wasn't Emmy to think of—and there
was no way she was going to leave her on her own overnight if she could help it—then Darcy knew the utmost
reluctance to go to Neve's home in Cornthorpe. But he
was waiting, waiting for her answer, and she knew she
had to be exceedingly tactful. She could ruin the
agency's chances of more work if she refused point
blank.

She tried, 'Er—we have several other secretaries on
our books, all of them very . . .' and was chopped off
with a no-nonsense:

'I want you.'

Darcy bit down the anger that started to rise. So he
was still keeping his eye on her, was still suspicious of
her.

'Correct me if I'm wrong,' he said, when she had made

no answer, 'but you did tell me, I believe, that the slogan of the outfit you work for is "Any job, Any time, Any place", didn't you?'

His silky sarcasm had to be taken. For Jane's sake she had to remember that this powerful man could be instrumental in making or breaking the agency.

'Why do I have to stay overnight?' If she had to do the job, and it didn't look as though she was going to wriggle out of it—what was she thinking of, turning down work the agency could do with anyway?—then she could drive home on Saturday and go back again on Sunday.

'Because . . .' Neve paused. She could almost hear him thinking why the hell should he give her a reason. She wasn't surprised when he added, '. . . I say so.'

She held back the urge to slam down the phone, then thought of Jane. She thought of Emmy—what was she up to in her bedroom?—and the thoughts of Emmy stayed.

'I—It's not—easy for me to be away from home overnight.'

'Why?' And his brain was not slow with calculations. 'You told me you lived alone.' And his voice fairly thundering now over the wires, he accused, 'You *are* living with someone!'

'It's not what you think,' she flashed back.

'Like hell it's not!'

There was nothing for it, she would have to tell him. It sounded as though any second now he would be the one to slam down the phone. Jane would never forgive her.

'If you must know,' she said, and the silence the other end told her he did, 'I live with—an elderly lady.' Silence still, and angrily she just knew he was thinking, pull the other one. 'I live with my mother's old nanny,' came from her against her will.

Silence again. Well, she just wasn't adding anything to that. Then she heard his voice again, grating, sarcastic, 'That's a new one. What size collar does *she* take?'

And that was just too much. 'You disbelieving swine!' she yelled down the phone. 'I was telling you the truth!' Her temper fled. She'd done it now, she thought, and could have groaned aloud. She would have to confess to Jane. Jane would . . .

'In that case you'd better bring *her* with you,' fell into her ear.

'Bring her . . .' she gasped.

'You know where I live. I'll expect you both tomorrow at ten sharp.'

'But . . .'

'Either you come for the weekend, Darcy,' he told her, surprising her that he used her first name when his tone was so aggressive, 'or the work I was planning to put Adaptable Temps' way won't come off.'

He had won, damn him. There was no way out of it. 'Very well,' she said quietly, and would have put down the phone; there was nothing further she wanted to say to him—nothing that wouldn't ruin the agency's chances for certain.

'And since I'll have to feed you,' he added, before she could carry out her intention, 'you'd better bring a dinner gown that won't shame me in front of my guests.'

Before she could slam the phone down she heard the click that meant his receiver had already been returned to its rest. Swine! Swine, swine, she fumed. Then suddenly she was feeling better. She'd have to put up with him while they were working, but if he had guests, she wouldn't have to suffer his solitary company at dinner.

She knew Emmy of old. Despite any pleading from her, brought up in the old school, she would think it was to be a formal gathering once she knew there were to be other people present, and would declare she would eat with the staff. Oh, that Darcy could do the same, but since Neve had made a point of mentioning she bring a dinner dress, she knew she hadn't a prayer. Now where was Emmy? What was it that was keeping her so fully occupied?

Darcy met her coming from her room. She looked well pleased with life. If she had a little secret, Darcy decided to let her keep it. 'I was just going to make some coffee. Ready for a drink, Emmy?' she asked.

'I'll have chocolate, dear,' said Emmy, going with her into the kitchen. 'Coffee keeps me awake if I drink it this time of night.'

Darcy got down the china cups and saucers Miss Emsworth insisted on using, when a beaker would have suited her quite well. Then, taking it slowly so as not to send her into a flap, she told her about the job she had to do in Cornthorpe over the weekend.

'It will mean staying at Mr Macalister's home on Saturday night, but you'll like that, won't you?' she smiled. 'If we leave just before nine . . .'

'But I can't go, dear,' said Emmy, her eyes looking worried.

Darcy had no doubts that she would soon take that worried look from her. But because Emmy sometimes got muddled up, she took it very gently. 'Why not, love?' she asked.

'Well, I won't go if you don't want me to, Darcy, but I am supposed to be going to Brighton at eight in the morning. I've just finished my packing.'

Oh, the poor dear! Darcy thought, knowing full well it was next Saturday Emmy was going to Brighton, not this. She hoped she wouldn't be too disappointed, but if Emmy had got it right before, she had definitely said she was going away four weeks on Saturday, which had to be next Saturday.

Treading very carefully, she said, 'I wouldn't dream of you not going. You've looked forward to it so much—Only I thought it was next Saturday you were going.'

'You can't remember everything, concentrating so hard on the work you do,' said Emmy, looking at her proudly, just as though in her view the Prime Minister had an easier task than Darcy. Then, starting to look confused, 'I'm sure it's tomorrow I go. Mrs Bricknell reminded me again at the club this afternoon to be sure to bring my medical card.'

'Look, love, why don't I go and give her a ring?' said Darcy, blaming herself that she had not contacted Mrs Bricknell before.

Emmy looked at her with anxious eyes when Darcy came from the phone. And seeing that anxiety, Darcy had to put aside what she was feeling.

'My mistake,' she said brightly. 'Mrs Bricknell had arranged for the coach to pick you up at eight tomorrow morning.'

'Thank goodness for that!' exclaimed Emmy in relief. 'For a moment there I was beginning to think I was going to have to unpack everything!'

Darcy had done nothing about looking out a dinner gown that wouldn't 'shame' Neve Macalister in front of his guests as she stood in the street the next morning and waved Emmy off on her week's holiday.

The coach out of sight, she hurried indoors, the thought that had last night plagued her returning. Neve was never going to believe a word she said, never going to believe there was such a person as her mother's old nanny—especially when she turned up without her.

At a quarter to nine she set off, the weekend case she had hurriedly packed reposing on the back seat. She was half way to Cornthorpe, at the point of no return, when the 'I'll show him' feeling left her. Oh, blow him, she thought, but it no longer seemed a good idea to try and make his eyes pop out that instead of bringing with her a dignified dinner gown, she had brought with her a dazzling red jump-suit. She'd have to wear it now, unless she went down to dinner in the trousers and shirt she was wearing. All she hoped was that none of his house guests were in the coronary belt.

She took a wrong turn after leaving the main road, and had gone several miles up a wrong road before she realised her mistake, so that her intention to arrive smack on the button of ten just didn't materialise.

At ten past ten she pulled up outside the large manor house she had hoped never to see again.

A manservant opened the door, bringing to her mind the last time she had been in Neve's home. There hadn't been a servant about the place then because Neve had sent them all away.

'My name's Darcy Alexander,' she said, and smiled because the manservant smiled, and she had no axe to grind with him.

'I'll take your case to your room, Miss Alexander,' he said, relieving her of it. 'Mr Macalister is expecting you. He said to show you the way to the study.'

So the staff weren't to have any inkling of what had gone on that time when they had been given an unexpected break! Darcy smiled, damping down the imp of mischief that would have had her telling him not to bother, that she knew the way, and trotted along beside him.

'Miss Alexander, sir,' he announced, then stood back, allowing Darcy into the room.

Neve, dressed casually in light sweater and slacks, allowed his eyes to travel over her. Then no sooner had his manservant closed the door than he was barking:

'You're late!'

'Pardon me for breathing,' she muttered, thought he was going to smile, and knew when he didn't that that had been too much to hope for, and said, 'I took a wrong turning.'

'Well, now you're here we'd better get on with some work.' He paused. 'No, you'd better go and see that the old lady is settled in first.'

It was considerate of him, she thought, and blushed guiltily, when she had nothing to feel guilty about. She had hoped to get in first with her explanation about Emmy going on holiday, the confusion about the dates, but didn't get the opportunity.

'You *did* bring the elderly lady with you?' he questioned, shrewdness there in his eyes, that alone telling her she was batting on a losing wicket.

'No,' she said, and still ready to explain, 'Because . . .'

'Because you were lying. Because there is no dear sweet old biddy,' he said contemptuously. And Darcy was made furious as much by his contempt as by the fact he never gave credence to anything she said. 'When you're ready,' he intimated sharply when she had made no move to explain or to sit down and start work.

'I'd like to wash my hands first,' she said, being perverse just for the pure hell of it. 'Do I show myself to my room—I believe I can remember which one it is.'

He threw down his pen in disgust and was on his feet saying, 'You're not in *that* room—follow me,' and leaving her trailing behind as he strode from the study.

He slowed when a thin woman in a navy dress appeared on the first floor landing, introducing her as his housekeeper, Mrs Gow. 'How do you do,' said Darcy pleasantly, then felt a jerk on her arm—Neve plainly telling her he hadn't got time to waste while she spent all day chatting to his housekeeper.

'You didn't think it necessary to send your staff away this weekend?' she asked with sugary innocence when he stopped and opened one of the doors, but was ignored as he led her into one of the prettiest bedrooms she had ever seen.

'What a lovely room!' she couldn't help exclaiming; there were white frills everywhere, lemon bedspread and bedroom chair, wallpaper with pale yellow rosebuds.

She looked at him, thought he looked pleased she liked it, and couldn't help but wonder if he had chosen this room for her. Then as she looked into his eyes and saw nothing but hardness there she knew he wasn't bothered about her opinion of the room, that Mrs Gow had been told any room would do for her, that he had probably been put out when he had learned that it was this particular room she had been allocated.

'Be down in five minutes,' he snapped brusquely.

Darcy glared at his departing back. She would like to have lingered in the room. Then she made herself think of the agency. She was here to work, wasn't she?

They got through a fair amount in the hours until lunch time, being able to go at a good pace without the constant interruptions of the office, where the telephone never stopped ringing.

Lunch was a light meal, and Neve did not seem disposed to linger over it, which suited Darcy quite well. Then it was back to work. He must have brought the typewriter from the office yesterday, she saw, recognising a mark on it that had been there when she had used it before, and she pounded steadily away on the machine until half past four when she pulled the last piece of typing from it.

Neve had been in a brutish mood ever since she had arrived, and his thinking she had lied to him about the existence of her mother's old nanny had not helped any. Not that she'd expected anything different. For her sins, he was ready to work her until she dropped.

With that thought still in her head, it accounted for her surprise when, after she had placed the typed matter before him, he suddenly said:

'That's it for today.'

Darcy checked her watch. 'It's only half past four. We could ...'

'Dinner is at eight,' she was informed. And he added, to her surprise, 'You've worked hard, you've earned a rest before dinner.'

Darcy wasn't sure her mouth didn't gape, this kindness in him was so unexpected. She went slowly to the door, but somehow it didn't seem right to leave him without another word. Without her wanting it to, his kindness had softened something in her.

'H-how about you?' she asked, and was caught by his piercing look and had to go on, already regretting she hadn't just walked out. 'I mean, are you going to have a break too?'

'You care?' he enquired. And although he didn't sound sarcastic, she was sure sarcasm must be there.

'You'd fall off your perch if I said yes,' she mocked flippantly.

He was hard-eyed again as she left him. 'Reckon I would,' he replied.

Darcy saw in her absence that someone had been to her pretty room and unpacked her things. Not that there was very much to unpack—her nightdress, fresh underwear, toilet things, and that garment she was to wear tonight.

She went to the wardrobe, opened the door on the single item it housed. It had seemed a good idea at the time, she thought, wishing she had brought something else with her rather than the flamboyant red jump-suit with its shoestring shoulder straps. She looked good in it, she knew she did. She had only had it on once, and that had been when she had tried it on in the shop. She just didn't go to places where she could wear it, but had bought it nevertheless, because she hadn't been able to resist it.

She closed the door on it. The die was cast, she had nothing else with her she could wear. She called, 'Come in,' in answer to the discreet knock on her door, and saw Mrs Gow enter bearing a welcome tray of tea.

'I could have come down and collected that,' she said. The housekeeper looked about sixty, while her legs were much younger.

'Mr Macalister thought you might appreciate some tea,' the housekeeper surprised her by saying, 'and it was no trouble.'

While the tray was being set down on a small rosewood table beside the lemon Dralon bedroom chair, Darcy remarked, to fill in the small moment of silence, 'Dinner is at eight, I believe Mr Macalister said.'

'That's right, Miss Alexander. Though Mr Macalister will want you to join him in the drawing room for a drink first, I daresay.'

Darcy smiled. Eight o'clock would be fine, she thought. Though perhaps she'd better get down earlier, in view of Neve's guests.

'Has anyone else arrived yet?' She hadn't seen anyone else, or heard anyone arriving, but they could have come while she had been pounding away on the typewriter.

Her question seemed to puzzle the housekeeper. And Darcy was just about to hope she hadn't forgotten other people were due for dinner—it would be short rations all round if she had—when light appeared to dawn for Mrs Gow.

'Mr Blair doesn't come home every weekend,' she smiled, and, letting her hair down since Darcy was proving not a bit standoffish, 'Sometimes he doesn't make it in the week either.'

Darcy had to smile at the implication behind that. And then Mrs Gow remembered she had something on the stove that should be looked at.

'There's a bell there,' she said, indicating the push button by the bedhead. 'If you need anything, please don't hesitate to ring.'

Darcy poured her tea, knowing she just wasn't into ringing bells and getting anyone up those stairs for anything she might need. She had learned nothing about any of Neve's guests, so perhaps they were only coming for dinner, not staying the weekend as she had thought. She did know one thing, though—Blair Macalister wouldn't be one among the dinner party tonight. And she was pleased about that. He'd have soon found out that his brother had no plans to trot up the aisle with her—if Neve hadn't put him right on that score already.

For no reason, that thought alone made her forget Neve had shown kindness in telling her to rest before dinner, had shown kindness in having tea sent up to her. She drank her tea, rested a while, then went to soak in the bath, and was back again to not liking Neve Macalister very much at all.

It was seven-forty-five when she stood before the mirror and was ready to go down. She had fifteen minutes in which to present herself downstairs. But, as Darcy stared at her reflection, she admitted she was nervous.

It was all the fault of the jump-suit, of course—and yet she really did look as good in it as she remembered.

It showed off her long length of leg, fell straight from bust to hips, but when she moved, the clinging jersey material somehow managed to show up the narrowness of her waist. With the shoulder straps being so very narrow it had been impossible to wear a bra. Not that she needed to wear one, she thought, her firm bust showed that. But she couldn't help thinking Emmy would have been horrified at her bra-less state. Darcy smiled through her nerves. What was she worrying about? Had she been around Emmy so long that she too had become old-fashioned? She was a modern girl, for goodness' sake. If she took heed of Emmy's advice, she would daily don fleecy underwear!

Darcy told herself she wasn't nervous, that she didn't need the comfort of gripping on to her brown leather handbag. It was just that she might need her hanky or something—and where in the jump-suit was there anywhere to stow a hanky?

At two minutes to eight she presented herself at the drawing room door. She listened, thought it odd that she couldn't hear a babble of voices, and hoped fervently that what quiet talk there must be wouldn't fall into a hush of astonishment when she walked in. The trouble was, being such a stay-at-home, she had got out of the way of mixing socially.

It was when she decided that she was every bit as good as Neve Macalister *and* his guests that Darcy ceased hesitating outside the door. Her chin tilted, she turned the handle and went in. Then she stopped, startled.

For the only person in the room, a glass in his hand, and looking superb in his dinner jacket, was Neve Macalister!

'Where are . . .' she began, but didn't get further. The openly admiring look in his eyes, as moving towards her they roved over her, sent flying from her mind all thought of what she had been going to say.

A few yards from her, Neve paused, a curve coming to that mouth that seldom smiled. 'You're beautiful,' he said softly, his admiration not waning.

Aware of her sudden flush of colour, Darcy fought against the something in her that wanted to smile back at his compliment. She tried hard to remember she didn't like him, and was overwhelmingly glad, when just at that moment, Mrs Gow popped her head round the door.

'We'll be there shortly,' Neve told his housekepper, his eyes not leaving Darcy, Mrs Gow's unspoken, 'Dinner is ready,' taken as read by him. 'Would you care for a drink before we have dinner, Darcy?' he asked pleasantly.

His pleasantness was another surprise. Or perhaps it wasn't, she thought. If his guests were already seated, good manners decreed that the two of them didn't enter the dining room throwing disgruntled looks at each other.

'Er—no, thanks,' she said belatedly. And thinking of the people in the dining room waiting, she edged towards the door—a hint Neve seemed to accept as meaning she wanted her dinner, as he reached the door first and held it open for her.

And then Darcy was not so much startled as shocked. For as she preceded him into the dining room, she saw that not another soul was present. And not only that, as her eyes went rapidly to the table, she saw from the place settings laid, only two, that there were not going to be any other people present. Because Neve Macalister just wasn't expecting any guests.

Stock still, she stood. She knew Neve was at her shoulder, looking down at her as though still liking what he saw. But that was not the reason that colour flooded into her face. She was furious.

'Which one of us is the bigger liar?' she blazed, swinging round to glare up into his eyes. 'Or,' she tried for calm, 'was it your sweet, charming disposition that put your guests off?'

And, calm nowhere near, her temper boiling over, shaking off the hand that came to her elbow, just as though he was going to ignore her fury and guide her to her seat at the table:

'Or,' she fired, 'did you think I might try my hand at blackmailing your guests? Is that why you cancelled your dinner party?'

CHAPTER EIGHT

READY to explode at whatever answer he gave, Darcy was struck dumb that not one word of her charge did he reply to. Instead, the charming disposition she had accused him of not having was suddenly there, and his smile turned into a very definite grin when softly, he said:

'Do you know, Darcy, you become even more beautiful when you're angry.' And as Mrs Gow came in behind them, 'Shall we take our seats? We seem to be blocking Mrs Gow's way.'

Respect for the housekeeper sent Darcy's intention not to budge on its way. Good manners decreed she couldn't let fly at Neve with Mrs Gow standing there.

'If you would like to sit here,' said Neve, pulling out a chair for her.

Reluctantly Darcy went forward, just waiting for the time when only the two of them were there, and she could again demand to know if he thought a girl like her should not be mixing with anyone he regarded as a friend.

A delicious smell of home-made soup assailed her nostrils as Mrs Gow served the first course. If anger hadn't negated all other senses, Darcy thought she might well be hungry. Mrs Gow was on her way from the room when Neve poured her a glass of wine and handed it to her.

Momentarily she forgot her anger as she watched those long sensitive fingers. His scraped knuckle had healed, she saw. Then she was again remembering she was a distrusted blackmailer.

But before she could angrily fire up at him again, Neve was taking the ground from under her, his smile no longer visible, his voice level as though he could not see she was still boiling, by saying:

'How's the agency doing these days? It was struggling at one time, I believe.'

It was deliberate—she knew that! He was aware of her fury, yet with a simple sentence or two, had flattened it.

Hostilely she looked across the table at him, and saw that not by a flicker of an eyelash was he revealing that to mention the agency was a surefire way to have her remembering her loyalty to Jane, remembering he was the one man she couldn't afford to upset. He was clearly telling her he was paying the piper, the tune was his, and she hadn't better forget it.

And because he was paying, she had to sit there and take it. She couldn't say a word in argument that given the choice she would have preferrred to have her meal on a tray in her room. She would love to have told him the agency weren't as desperate for work as she had once told him they were.

But she had to swallow hard on her ire before she spoke. 'As you know,' she said, still quietly seething, 'at this stage of the agency's development, we're prepared to take on any job.' She couldn't hide the sarcasm, but tried to cover it with a false smile as she added, 'Even jobs we know are going to be loathsome.' She began to feel better for having got that dig in.

But Neve did not rise to her remark. He was intent on being the perfect host she saw, although she was going to make sure Jane left him in no doubt that if he wanted Darcy Alexander for his dinner companion, he would have to pay for her time.

Neve, it appeared, had never been in any doubt that he was going to be charged for every hour she spent in his company. His next remark told her so, though he was frowning as he brought it out.

'Do you often dine with an agency client?'

Darcy spooned soup to her mouth. It really was delicious. She took another spoonful, then looked across the table. His soup was going cold while he waited for her answer. 'You're the first,' she said, and didn't watch to see what he made of that as she again dipped into her bowl and caught a glimpse of his spoon, as he did the same.

With the second course, roast beef with all the trimmings, Neve served a different wine, and the conversation was bitty while Mrs Gow was in the room. When the housekeeper departed, however, he casually brought the conversation back to Darcy, asking had she any plans she'd had to cancel in order to work for him that weekend.

She hadn't had a thing planned. Probably a walk with Emmy tomorrow, had Emmy not gone to Brighton. And she really had to get down to that French study. But although she doubted his query was as casual as he'd made it sound, she couldn't see any reason for not answering honestly.

'No,' she replied, 'I'd nothing special arranged.'

She lifted her eyes then and saw that his eyes were on her. 'You didn't have a boy-friend you had to put off?' He seemed mildly surprised, and it irritated her. It appeared to her there wasn't one darn thing she could say that he wouldn't question.

'I—don't have a lot of time for boy-friends,' she told him shortly.

'You can't be working all the time,' he said, just as though she thought, when not working, he thought men would be queuing up at her door to take her out.

'I study a lot.' The rein on her temper was growing shorter and shorter. And to prevent his next question, 'I need to know a bit about everything in the work I do.'

'What are you studying at the moment?'

Darcy cut into a roast potato. It had sounded a sincere question, she thought, her anger cooling. Perhaps he wasn't discounting everything she said after all. Perhaps the fault lay with her, that it was she who was on edge because of her thoughts about why there were not other people present.

'I'm studying French,' she said. And, giving a little, 'Should the day ever come when we get the call for a bilingual secretary, then I want to be ready for it.'

That led him to ask what other jobs she had been called upon to do. And feeling more relaxed suddenly, Darcy opened up a little further, telling him about a pregnant whippet she had been called upon to dig-sit in case it decided to whelp while its owners were out.

'No problem there,' she remembered. 'I had the telephone number of the vet, with instructions to ring him at the first sign.'

And encouraged by him, the talk came easier to her; the wine she had sampled was helping her unwind, she thought, though the charm she denied he had was there as he drew her out. She went on to tell him about routine office jobs that had come her way, a book-keeping job she had tackled, and about the social secretary job she had once done for a fortnight.

They were at the end of their main course when just having told him about the waitressing job she had done in a racy type of club, the recollection of that job had her brow wrinkling.

Darcy laid down her knife and fork, her look of distaste showing as she recalled the two lecherous clients who had thought a waitress was fair game when they felt the urge to grab someone.

Why she happened to flick a glance at Neve just then, she had no idea, but her glance stayed with him—stayed with the latent aggression she saw there in the thrust of his jaw as those piercing dark eyes looked into her own that were still clouded over from that distasteful memory.

'Why the hell do you have to take jobs like that?' he asked roughly, for all the world as though he could tell she had hated working in that particular establishment. 'You're a damned good secretary, you could get a better paid job anywhere.'

She looked quickly away, hoping he couldn't see she didn't want to answer, and was saved having to reply

when Mrs Gow came in to clear away and serve the
final course.

'If you'd like to bring the coffee in,' Neve addressed
his housekeeper, 'we'll help ourselves.'

That was thoughtful of him, Darcy found herself
thinking. It must have been a long day for Mrs Gow.
Quite possibly she had rested in between, and was
probably well paid for her services. But that kindness in
him she had occasionally seen was there again that he
had told his housekeeper he saw nothing wrong in
having to pour his own coffee.

In the event it was Darcy who poured the coffee; her
appetite filled, she had only room for the smallest por-
tion of blackcurrant pie and cream.

She had started to get uptight when Neve had asked
her why she wasn't working permanently as a secretary.
And to forestall him should he remember there was an
answer outstanding, she quickly inserted a comment on
how good the pie was.

It appeared he wasn't bothered about his answer, and
feeling complimented that he thought her a 'damn good
secretary', she grew relaxed; she hadn't fancied telling
him that all her 'permanent' secretarial jobs had ended
in dismissal.

Her feeling of wellbeing grew as Neve told her about
the many fruit bushes that grew at the bottom of the
kitchen garden; of how Mrs Gow painstakingly picked
the blackcurrants and deep-froze them every July.

That left her wanting to ask how long Mrs Gow had
been with him. It sounded as though she had been with
him for years. Which must mean, she thought whimsically, that he wasn't the tyrant at home that he was at
the office. That also put it in her mind to wonder how
long Avril Knight had been with him. Did he change
his secretary every time he bought a new pair of shoes?

She smiled at her whimsy, and looked up to see there
was a pleasant look on Neve's face for her. Stupidly,
she realised later, she still smiled, in no way prepared
that having got her relaxed again, obviously not missing

that she hadn't wanted to answer his previous question, he chose that moment to ask:

'Why *do* you work for the agency, Darcy?'

'I . . .' she began, and was stumped.

'I accept that you have a tremendous loyalty to Jane Davis,' he said. And, making her eyes go wide, 'I admire you for it.'

Shaken by what he had just said, Darcy continued to stare at him. Neve Macalister had admitted, apart from the male in him appreciating her outer covering, that he actually admired something in her! She saw his eyes narrow suddenly and knew his clever brain was at work; and she was tense again.

'You haven't always done agency work, have you?' he asked, which seemed to call for a yes or no answer.

For a moment Darcy thought to lie. He never believed what she said anyway, so why bother with the truth?

'What work did you do before you joined Adaptable Temps?' he pressed.

'Er——' Her chance to give him a false 'Yes' had gone. 'I trained as a secretary.' She wanted to leave it there; she knew she was drowning. She just knew his questioning wouldn't stop there, but she just didn't want him to know any more. He wouldn't appreciate how she had felt when, however politely put, each job had ended the same way.

'After your training you worked as a secretary?' He had guessed rightly. She had known that he would. A nod was all the confirmation she gave him. 'Who for?'

Stubbornly she refused to answer. Why should she tell him anything? It was nothing to do with him what she had done in the past.

'You have something to hide?' he queried, suspicion glinting in his eyes. And that suspicion needled her— needled her into throwing caution to the wind.

'I worked for several employers,' she said, getting snappy. 'And if by "something to hide" you're asking did I get caught pilfering, then no, I didn't.' Then she saw he was too clever by half, as rapidly he fired:

'There's an intimation there that you were asked to leave, though.' And, stern-faced, not a bit abashed at asking the question, 'Were you sacked from any of them?'

On being driven into a corner, defiance was all she had for a weapon. 'If you must know, yes—yes, I was—from all of them.' That suspicion was still there, and she hated it. 'But not for what you're thinking,' she flashed. 'I wasn't sent on my way for trying to blackmail my employers.'

She had thought she was furious enough to jump to her feet and dash to her room, furious enough to go to her room and stay there until it was time to start work tomorrow morning. She even did cast her eyes about, looking for her bag ready to snatch it up. It annoyed her that she couldn't see it. She must have left it in the drawing room, though she couldn't remember having put it down in there. And her eyes showed her sparking anger as she looked at him about to leave.

Then she got another shock to see the suspicion she had thought she had seen in his eyes had gone, that the stern look had left him. And that if she wasn't very much mistaken, he was trying his hardest to be reasonable.

'So tell me about it,' he said quietly, and with that suggestion of a curve to his mouth, he coaxed, 'Tell me, Darcy, why, when as I said before, you're an excellent secretary, have several employers felt able to dispense with your services?'

She hesitated. She didn't want his good opinion of her. She was quite sure she could do without it even if he had just promoted her from 'a damn good secretary' to an 'excellent' one. Then suddenly she knew she was lying to herself. Oh, it had nothing to do with the back-handed way Neve had complimented her on her work—keeping his compliments to himself when she had worked in his office—but whether she liked it or not, it came home to her all at once that she did want his opinion of her to be good. That he had a good opinion of her was suddenly important.

'I . . .' she began, and floundered for a while. Then, when Neve made no move to hurry her, somehow she found the words. 'My—attendance record wasn't very good.'

'You find difficulty in getting up in the morning?' he asked, and didn't wait for her reply as he went on. 'Apart from being an understandable fifteen minutes late this morning, you've never been late while working for me.'

So he understood that had it not been for taking a wrong turn, bearing in mind he had led her out that time before, that she would have been there at ten. Why couldn't he have been like this when she had arrived? she wondered. The day would have got off to a much better start if he'd shown some understanding then.

'It wasn't that I was often late,' she explained, 'but—er—that some days, some weeks, I—er—often didn't go in at all,' and saw him considering what she had said, before, as though he was thinking aloud, he said:

'You're far from being lazy,' causing her to warm to him for that remark. Then he was questioning, 'Didn't you like the work you were doing? Were you bored?'

'Sometimes,' she admitted. And because all at once there seemed to be harmony in the room, no aggression, more kindness coming through than aggression, she found herself telling him, 'But it wasn't that. You remember the elderly lady I told you I live with?'

'The one you forgot to bring with you.' About to tighten up again, Darcy threw him a fiery look and met nothing but his bland smile, so that again tension was sent on its way. 'Your mother's nanny?' he added mildly.

'That's right,' she agreed. 'Well, since we came to London she's suffered with chest trouble. It usually starts in October and recurs on and off until about March, sometimes longer.' Her voice tailed off as she added, 'When she's not well, I take time off to look after her.'

He looked at her sharply, with scepticism, she thought, making her regret she had told him anything.

'Would it not be simpler to send her to hospital?'

His suggestion annoyed her. 'Emmy is eighty-two. She hates hospitals. And if your next bright suggestion is that I should put her in an old people's home, then don't bother. Emmy fears that more than she hates hospitals.'

'Meantime you can't hold down a job because, devoted to the old biddy as you undoubtedly are,' was he being sarcastic, was he still not believing a word she said? 'you prefer to let down the people who employ you.'

'Emmy is family—not related, but family,' Darcy flared. 'And I don't have to worry about letting down employers either any more. Because since Jane has taken me on her books, it doesn't matter if I'm unable to leave Emmy, another temp can take the job.'

'You have a private income?'

The question might have been a natural one seeing that if she wasn't working, she wasn't getting paid either. But, already annoyed at suspecting he thought she was lying her head off, Darcy did not see the question as natural.

'I don't supplement my income by blackmail!' she flashed.

'That wasn't what I asked,' came the maddeningly mild reply.

Looking mutinous, Darcy decided there and then to let him have the lot. Let him decide for himself if she had a private income!

'My father had a furniture business. I suppose you could say we were comfortably off—he didn't want me to train for any sort of work anyway. But I wanted to, and was glad I did. His business crashed. It was in trouble before he died, only I didn't know that until afterwards.'

Speaking of the father she loved had weakened her anger. And she wondered why she bothered anyway.

Neve was in no hurry to say anything, as, inspecting her empty cup, he took time out to pour them both another cup of coffee before he spoke.

'So when you're not working, things are tight?' he queried at last.

She darted him a suspicious glance of her own. If he was intimating ... She took a deep breath and decided to take his question at face value.

'We manage. Emmy has her state pension.'

'Why didn't she come with you today? She can't be ill or you wouldn't have left her—even for Jane Davis's sake.'

That sounded so much as though he considered she had been truthful in everything she had told him, that suddenly the mutiny in Darcy's soul disappeared. A smile even peeped out as she remembered:

'Emmy was in her bedroom for ages last night. I was just going in to see if she was all right—she gets a bit confused sometimes—then you rang. After your call I told her we were coming here for the weekend, and it was then she told me she'd been packing to go on a week's holiday today with this club she belongs to.' Her smile was a definite one as she said, 'Between us we were both confused. Emmy had told me about her holiday that Sunday I returned from being here. It could be that I was the one who wasn't thinking straight,' she added, 'but I thought it was next Saturday she was going to Brighton.'

She had been open with Neve, held nothing back. She had thought he was beginning to trust her. But one look at his hard expression as she came to the end was enough to tell her that not only was he not trusting her, but also that he didn't trust truth to be in a word of what she had just said. And when she didn't want it to—that caused her pain. Pain that all she had said had served only to remind him of the reason he had had for having her in his home that first time.

'Was it this Emmy you were on the phone to when I caught you?' he asked coldly, confirmation there that he was remembering that other time. 'Was it she you were calling "darling"—or was it someone else?'

It was at that juncture that Darcy did what she had thought of doing some fifteen minutes before. Pride had her not showing how it hurt to have told him all that and not be believed.

'What's it to you?' she asked, and was on her feet without waiting for his answer.

Tears were in her eyes as she hurried from the dining room. Tears, reminding her of her handkerchief, her bag. What sort of a man was he? she sniffed, as she went into the drawing room searching for her bag, hoping she felt more in control when she saw him again tomorrow morning, hating that he had got to her.

Grabbing at her bag, knowing she had been more nervous than she had thought, to have dropped it on the floor where she had found it, without even knowing she had done so, Darcy turned to leave the drawing room and go up to her room.

Surprise stopped her going a step further. Neve Macalister wasn't where she had left him. He was not still in the dining room finishing his coffee as she had supposed. He was there at the door she had left open, his tall frame blocking the doorway.

Darcy swallowed her tears, not wanting him to know he had the power to affect her in the slightest, but she could do nothing about the shine of tears in her eyes as she moved forward.

'What's the matter?'

Didn't he know? She felt ready to hit him for being so obtuse. Then she decided it was far better he didn't know—the whole of it, that was—she had herself only just realised it *all*.

'Let me pass,' she answered woodenly.

But he made no move to get out of her way. And suddenly she was desperate. She didn't want him to see her in tears, tears that were still threatening—didn't want him to see what his distrust could do to her.

Hopeful that if she again stepped forward he would

do the gentlemanly thing and move to one side, Darcy
went forward. She was right up to him when she found
to her consternation that the only movement he made
was to take hold of her upper arms.

Weakness invaded at his touch, set her insides quiver-
ing. Wanting badly to pull away, she was further
dismayed to find that weakness growing, rooting her
where she stood as slowly his hands stroked up and
down her upper arms.

She lifted her eyes, wanted to say something short
and snappy, but saw his gaze was on her shoulders,
shoulders he had once seen red from his fierce grip. The
bruises had gone now, but as his gaze stayed where only
thin straps covered her shoulders, words came dragged
from him, just as though he could see those bruises.

'I—don't want to—hurt you.'

Darcy didn't want her voice husky, but it was. 'Then
don't—please don't hurt me.' But he already had. And
she was powerless to avoid what must result in further
hurt, when, with a stifled groan, he gathered her in his
arms.

He did not kiss her. And for how long he held her,
gently, just like that in his arms, she could not have
said. But it was bliss to rest her head against his chest,
bliss to hear his heart pounding as her heart was
pounding. She knew she would have to break away soon
and go to her room, but some magic was binding her to
him as she felt sensitive fingers smoothing her hair. She
would break away—but not just yet.

When she felt the caress of his kiss by her left eyebrow,
she knew now she must leave him, and raised her head
as she tried to find some stiffening in her.

Her green-brown eyes met smouldering dark eyes. But
if he read in her look that she was about to go, the way
his arms tightened at the back of her told her he wasn't
going to make it easy for her.

Hypnotised by him, she found it impossible to make
that move to struggle out of his hold. Then she heard her
name come hoarsely from him. 'Darcy,' he said. And as

if tormented beyond endurance, 'Oh, Darcy, you're driving me mad!'

She thrilled at his tone, even if she didn't understand just why exactly she was driving him mad. But with those burning eyes fixed on hers, it went entirely from her mind that she had intended to go to her room. What was in her mind was the remembrance of his mouth on hers that time he had kissed her. And she could not deny she wanted to feel his lips on hers again.

What showed in her eyes that made Neve's mouth curve in a hint of a smile, she had no idea. But there was no thought in her mind, when all hint of a smile faded and his head came nearer, of not meeting him.

Gently at first, almost fleetingly, Neve's mouth, neither hard nor harsh as she had many times seen it, rested against hers, then transferred to bestow light kisses over her face, his lips touching her eyes, her cheeks.

When he brought his mouth back to claim hers, a sigh left Darcy, his kiss—longer, deeper—setting her heart hammering as mindlessly she clung to him.

For timeless moments Neve held her in the circle of his arms, his mouth saluting hers again and again, each kiss deeper than the one before, drawing, firing in her a yearning—a yearning that grew in him at her unrestrained response.

Her arms were round him when his mouth left hers to trail kisses down her throat. And her hands went to his neck where his dark hair touched his collar, a trembling starting inside her as her hands on his skin, at his hair, had Neve pressing her body to him.

The trembling in her increased as she felt the hardness of his body so close—so close to hers as he moved her yet nearer, claiming her lips once more, his mouth mobile, his need to have her pressed to him as his kiss lengthened, awakening in Darcy a need of her own to be even closer, a wild longing surging through her.

When his fingers caressed to her spine, she took her lead from him, her hands going beneath his jacket, her body on fire for him at the feel of his body heat. Her fingers moved over his back the way his were caressing her spine, feeling his convulsive movement at the first touch of her hands.

And when he raised his head and looked down into her flushed face, Darcy felt she had no need to answer the ragged, 'I want you,' that left him.

There was no thought in her of holding back as Neve picked her up in his arms and carried her to the deep and wide couch. His arms left her only briefly as he did away with his dinner jacket. Then he was there with her, lying there beside her on the couch.

Darcy was not thinking at all when she felt his body against hers. All thought had gone as their legs entwined, Neve's arms came round her, his mouth taking hers, the passion in him stirring a passion in her she had never experienced before.

His eyes went to her face when he broke the kiss, then on to her shoulders that had known his bruising. But there was nothing bruising about him now, as oh, so very gently, his hands caressed where once they had crushed. Tenderly they soothed away all memory of how brutal he had once been. Darcy had never dreamed a man, a man like Neve, could be so gentle.

His eyes came back to her face, to her inviting lips, and as if that invitation was irresistible, Neve kissed her. And this was something else again. While they had been standing, just before he had carried her to the couch, she had known what was going to happen. But the passion, the intensity in that kiss, had her knowing that there was no going back now.

And she didn't want to go back. She wanted Neve to make love to her. There could be no other outcome if he was feeling the way she was, and she knew that he was.

But she couldn't help the flutter of panic that hit her when, his mouth left hers, his hands and eyes returned to her shoulders as without haste he removed first one dainty shoulder strap down and then the other.

'Neve!' she choked.

Bringing his look back to her eyes, she saw the question his were asking—why had she called his name? It might have been in her mind to tell him she hadn't been in this enchanted land he had taken her to before, but she wasn't sure of anything any more. And as his eyes stayed with her, all she knew was that if she said anything at all about the foreign terrain she was in, then she might find her passport to paradise and beyond had been confiscated.

'Nothing,' she said, and smiled. It was a giving smile. Then Neve kissed her—kissed her while his hands caressed her shoulders.

Their bodies still touching, his eyes were afire with desire as they looked into hers, when she felt his hands on the zip of her jump-suit. She felt the material pulled back from her breasts, and her colour, already pink, flushed a deep red.

Neve observed it, but although he looked fractionally puzzled, he did not question it. His eyes left hers and she choked, 'I . . .' not knowing what she wanted to say, shyness having the word escaping as his eyes went to her uncovered breasts.

Then his hands and lips were caressing her, and she was fighting to oust that shyness. Shyness fighting a battle with the wild rapturous urgings the touch of his lips aroused as they caressed her breasts.

And then as his body came over hers, nothing else mattered. She wanted him. Even not knowing of her shyness, he was sending it away. She wanted him. He wanted her. She knew it, even before he repeated the words, said it out loud, her senses were telling her so.

'I want you, Darcy,' he breathed. 'God, how I want you!' She smiled, enraptured, wanting to tell him she wanted him too. Then she was to wish he had said nothing more, for he kissed her again, knowing she was all his, and breathed softly, 'Let's make this a weekend we shall never forget.'

And that for Darcy at that time was the cruellest thing

anyone had ever said to her. For, desperately wanting him as she did, that sentence awakened common sense that had fallen asleep from the moment he had taken her in his arms.

She stiffened in his hold. She wanted to tell her common sense to go to sleep again, but it would not. It had come roaring awake. Was nagging at her, insisting on being heard, was telling her that it was only for this weekend that Neve wanted her. He had just said so hadn't he?

He was still over her, making it impossible for her to flee. But as she struggled to find her thin shoulder straps, struggled to get her top from around her waist and back covering her, she had to realise that by his very wording 'a weekend we shall remember' the giving, taking, the sharing of their bodies, would be isolated in his memory of her—her as a person.

'Your zip sticking in you?' he asked, his voice soft, still that of a lover, as the way she was struggling with her top got through the heat of his desire. He moved, his hands going to the material too, pulling it down, not up, as if the best way in his view out of the dilemma was to take the garment from her completely.

'Don't!' she exclaimed croakily, embarrassment added to the rest of her emotions as she saw, as he must, the naked flatness of her belly, the top of her white bikini briefs on view with her jump-suit well down her hips.

'Don't?' She heard the smile that entered his voice as in surprise, as though not quite believing it, he added, 'You're not shy, are you, Darcy?'

He had looked to be fascinated by her hips, but as his eyes travelled slowly upwards, lingering on her pink-tipped swollen breasts, then up to her face, he could see for himself that the colour there was not just the flush of a woman about to be joined in love.

'I don't want to—go any further,' she said, crying, bleeding inside, then some last vestige of pride came, making it impossible to tell him now of her innocence, making her not wanting him to know that while he might briefly remember the weekend on odd occasions, she would never forget it.

'I thought we'd gone past the joking stage,' he said quietly, that something in his tone telling her he just wasn't believing that she could be serious, not at this last moment.

Darcy could not remember the joking ever starting. But Neve had moved sufficiently for her to pull her jump-suit up, to hold the top in front of her, to cover her breasts from his view.

'I don't want to,' she said stubbornly, wishing he would move from the outside edge of the couch. She just wasn't up to an undignified scramble over the top of him; always supposing his hands, that had been gentle, didn't turn hard and she was hauled back.

She knew he was looking into her face, but kept her eyes lowered. 'You're lying, Darcy,' she heard him say quietly. 'You want me as I want you. I know you do.'

It seemed to her then that he was always accusing her of not being truthful. And she was glad of the anger she felt then. Because she was nowhere near certain, feeling as vulnerable as she did, that had she not felt angry, then regardless of the pain she would suffer afterwards if he refused to take heed, began to kiss her again, she might give in.

'I've said I don't want you to make love to me, and that's—that's an end to it,' she said, her voice going out of control. She conquered her panic that he might not listen to her, and asked woodenly, 'Will you let me get up, please?'

He moved, but only just enough to allow her to sit up; her legs were still on the couch. Neve sat too, but was still barring her way, his eyes not revealing anything as she righted her shoulder straps, glanced at him and hurriedly away.

'What's wrong?'

'Can't you accept that—that—that I d-don't want to go . . .'

'But you did. You wanted to go all the way,' he told her bluntly.

'Well, I've—I've changed my mind,' she said, hating this conversation. Suddenly hating him that he just wouldn't let her go without having to have this post mortem.

She had no intention of letting him dissect any of her reasons, and when he moved again, she managed to swing her legs off the couch, glad to find the floor solid beneath her feet.

She made to stand, then felt his hand firm on her arm, and knew she just wasn't going anywhere until he had got to the bottom of what had changed her from a yielding, pliant woman to this frigid creature who wouldn't even look at him.

She dared another glance, knew his mind was ticking over, but could read nothing of what he was thinking. Though she wished with all her heart she had not shown him, except for those two moments when shyness had gripped, that she was eager to go wherever he led.

And then she had the terrible idea that he was back-tracking over their lovemaking, was remembering her moments of shyness—overlooked at the time. And she knew positively, when a sudden stunned look crossed his face, that he was remembering something else.

That stunned expression was still there in his eyes, disbelief too, when letting go her arm he kept hold of her by placing a hand to the side of her face, turning her so he could see into her eyes.

'You—once told me you were a virgin,' he said, to her despair, then promptly sent despair on its way by rousing her anger that he just wouldn't—*wouldn't* believe a thing she told him, by asking, 'You're not—are you?'

She pulled away from him, jumping to her feet, the only passion about her now the passion of anger.

'When have you ever believed anything I've said?' she stormed, more bruised than from any physical injury he could do her. 'You wouldn't believe me if I said I was, would you? You'd question it, decide I was lying.' She wanted to cry that the beautiful loving they had shared had ended like this, and rejected tears as the thought came; her passport had been one to a fool's paradise— only she thinking it beautiful, while to him she was just another woman.

'Are you?' He was on his feet too, still questioning, still not believing.

'There's only one way to find out,' she said, wanting to hit him for his insensitivity. 'But since I've told you I don't want—t-to, you're never going to know, are you?'

From the look of him she thought he was going to take hold of her. She saw he looked shaken, and was glad, as she backed a step, that she had found that strength to reject him.

Neve didn't take that step that would have brought him up to her. But he was still looking stunned as the words left him, 'You damn well *are!*' just as though he still wasn't believing it.

And that made her madder than ever, had her in her anger hurling dreadful things at him so he shouldn't see her hurt. Things she knew just weren't true. But as she saw it then—why bother with the truth?—he discounted it at every step.

'Our slogan "Any job" has obviously given you the wrong impression,' she told him angrily. 'We just aren't into the work you have in mind!'

She saw the narrowing of his eyes, and knew, as she went on hellbent, that this wasn't going to be a one way fight. But she was past caring, as, lying in her teeth, she went on.

'Of course, since knowing you, I realise no female would willingly share your bed, but . . .'

It was as far as she got. She had drawn the heat of his anger, and without moving, he very soon cut her down to size as he retorted:

'As I recall it, you were seven eighths of the way there without me having to exert myself too much.'

She had no answer to that, and was hating him that in answer to her lies, his truth was a sturdier combat

weapon. 'Loyalty to the firm,' she lied—Jane and letting
her down had been nowhere in her head when she had
been on that couch with him. 'But the fee you'll be
charged was never intended to include—er—that sort of
thing.'

Darcy knew as soon as the words left her that such
talk had offended him. She knew it even before the ice
in him began to form. It was hot ice, and she was soon
to know that when it came to using offensive words,
then Neve could hurt far worse than she ever could.

'Forgive my lack of perspicacity in asking you about
your financial position,' he said, his voice silky, at odds
with the ice in his eyes. 'I've only just realised the obvious—the way in which you supplement your income.'
And while she was gasping that he couldn't be inferring
what he was actually inferring, he gave her a grim look
though was still speaking in those same silky tones, as
he asked, 'How much do you *usually* charge?'

Pain, hurt, even though she had started this sort of
talk, exploded in her. Searing rage erupted through the
crippling words he had tossed at her, and in an instant
she had closed the gap between them and hit him a
cracking blow across the side of his face.

But even as her hand was swinging away from him,
Neve had grabbed hold of her wrist. 'You . . .' he bit,
and Darcy flinched, for the look of fury in him told her
he was going to hit her back.

'Isn't hitting me once enough for you?' she yelled,
real fear welling up inside her.

She saw his jaw clench at the memory of the time she
had grown hysterical, and of the similar offering he had
served her. And then, to her amazement, all anger left
him. Suddenly he looked defeated. But when he let go
her wrists and turned his back on her, she wasn't waiting
around for anything. Darcy ran from the room.

Never more hurt in her life by the terrible thing he
had said to her, she raced up the stairs, was in her
room grabbing at her suitcase, thrusting her belongings
into it any old how.

She knew she had to go back to the drawing room to collect her bag—she hadn't stopped for anything when she had fled—and had it not held her car keys, she wouldn't have bothered.

Wiping her eyes, she knew she just couldn't stay here. She *couldn't*. Never did she want to see Neve again. She felt used up. There was no strength in her to renew hostilities.

Ten minutes later, her weekend case in hand, she retraced her steps downstairs, the sound of her feet deadened by the thick carpeting. At the bottom of the stairs she glanced along the hall. There was no light coming from beneath the drawing room door—but there was a light from under the door of the study.

So that was how much it meant to him! A blazing exchange with his weekend secretary, then forget it, he had work to do.

Noiselessly Darcy collected her bag from the drawing room. Noiselessly she went to the front door. And noiselessly, she opened it and went out to her car.

CHAPTER NINE

PERHAPS it was just as well Emmy was away, Darcy thought, when she dragged herself out of bed on Sunday morning and saw her red-rimmed eyes. She wasn't up to any of Emmy's questions. Padding to the kitchen, she made a cup of coffee and sat there drinking it, thinking.

She was in love with Neve Macalister, of course. She had been for some time, only she just hadn't wanted to face it. She didn't want to face it now. But it was there, as it had been last night, and wouldn't go away.

Moodily she stared into her cup, remembering his, 'Oh, Darcy, you're driving me mad.' She knew now, of course, what he had meant. He had not forgotten the way they had lain on her bed and kissed after he had hit her either. With her sitting opposite him at dinner, just the top of her jump-suited bra-less figure visible, desire for her body must have been stirring even while they ate.

She recalled the vile things he had said that had earned *him* a smack on the face. She had said some pretty awful things too, she recalled, so perhaps it was all even Steven.

Darcy couldn't help wondering during the afternoon at what time Neve had discovered she had walked out. It would not have been last night. Fifteen minutes after she had slapped him he had already been buried in his work. She wondered how long he had sat at his desk this morning waiting for her to appear before telling someone to go and tell her to hurry up. But it was only as she was cogitating on the answer to that that the realisation of what she had done struck home.

Horrified, she realised what in effect she had actually done. The work yesterday had been real enough—no pretext about that. And she—she had walked out on the job! Walked out on an influential employer of the agency's services! Hot on the heels of that calamitous realisation came the remembrance of Neve's phone call on Friday, came memory of the condition for him putting more work the agency's way; that condition that she stayed and worked for him not for just one day, but for the whole weekend!

For the next half hour she toyed with the idea of ringing Jane. She decided against it. What could she tell her? That she could forget the hopes she had that through Macalister Precision Equipment the agency was on its way because she had taken a swipe at the head of that company, and had walked out on the job? She couldn't do it, couldn't tell anyone what it was that had led up to her hitting him.

Darcy went to bed that night, and shed more tears. It was useless trying to stop her mind from thinking of Neve; he was seldom from her.

Tomorrow, she thought, having a try anyway, she would have to ring Jane. She had said she would to see if any work had come in for her. Though she hoped Neve Macalister's name wouldn't come up—she felt guilty enough about snookering the agency's chances without having her conscience prodded if Jane mentioned his name. He was there again in her head.

After a dreadful night, Darcy got up on Monday wondering if she would have slept better if she wasn't carrying a load of guilt about what she had done to Jane's hopes.

At nine the thought occurred that perhaps she should ring Neve and beg him not to go back on his promise to put some work Jane's way. But instantly she rejected it. No way was she going to ring him and . . . At a quarter past nine she was dithering, a picture of Jane, of little Edward, coming between her and her loathing of the very idea.

At half past nine she dialled. She got through to Avril Knight, who then put her through to Neve.

'Darcy?' His voice was gritty, as though he had been

absorbed in some complicated figure work. But he wasn't tearing into her as she suspected he might.

'I'm—I'm sorry to interrupt your day.' Just to hear him again had her stammering. 'B-but I wanted— to ask you something.'

'I'm sorry too,' she heard, 'for what I said on Saturday.'

His apology, grittily uttered, was so unexpected, Darcy didn't have an answer. She swallowed, then said hurriedly, 'W-we both said th-things we didn't mean.'

'You're going to forgive me?'

Wanting to melt, to say yes, loving him as she did she would forgive him anything, she knew suddenly that it wouldn't matter a tinker's cuss to him whether she forgave him or not.

'Of course,' she said, the softness going from her voice. And getting in there while she had the courage, 'What I rang you for actually, was—er——' She stopped, her palms sweating. 'Well, I know I should have worked for you yesterday and didn't . . .'

'You want to come to the office today?'

'Oh no.' She shied from that, even if it did mean Avril Knight was going to be snowed under typing back the work he had done after she had gone. 'I just wanted to know if you were . . .' she licked dry lips, 'if you intended to hold it a-against the agency,' her voice faltered at the silence the other end, 'that I—walked out,' she made herself finish.

Then it was not silent at the other end. Neve's voice came snarling down the wires, the moment before his phone was banged down.

'Your high opinion of me will keep me sleepless!' he barked.

Darcy replaced the phone, wanting to cry again. It was *his* good opinion of her she wanted—and so much more.

She took several minutes to get herself under control; she still didn't know whether Neve was going to go back on his word, then she picked up the phone again and dialled the agency.

'Hello, Darcy,' said Jane cheerfully. 'Got something for you for tomorrow. Just a minute while I get the card.'

'You sound cheerful,' remarked Darcy, groaning inwardly that Jane might not be cheerful for much longer.

'I have everything to be cheerful about,' Jane chirruped. 'Edward is coming out of hospital tomorrow, and—guess what?'

It had to be something good by the sound of it, but Darcy wasn't up to guessing games that morning. 'Tell,' she said. 'Don't keep me in suspense.'

Jane tried to hang it out, but couldn't for longer than two seconds. 'At precisely five minutes past nine this morning,' she came rushing in, 'I had a call from Macalister Precision Equipment!'

Darcy's heart sank. Her first reaction was one of hurt, of deep disappointment. She had no cause to feel so wounded, she knew that. She had fully expected Neve to ring the agency and blast them for one of their unreliable staff walking out on him ... Her thoughts stopped there, puzzlement surmounting her hurt. Jane wouldn't be cheerful if ...

'N-Neve Macalister rang?' she enquired hesitantly.

'No, not him. But on his instructions, his personnel department. Incidentally, I understand you worked for him over the weekend, I've been told to send my account in for Saturday and Sunday.'

Tears, laughing crying tears, tears that Neve hadn't warranted going down in her estimation, were in Darcy's eyes. Tears that he was above being small-minded, even if it left him out of pocket. Even if it had him paying for Sunday work she hadn't done.

But Jane was going on; the weekend work she had done, or was supposed to have done, was a side issue. 'What Mr Harris, the personnel manager, really rang for was to ask for a couple of typists for their typing pool.' Jane's excitement got out of hand as she joyfully said, 'The agency is on its way, Darcy—it's on its way!'

Darcy could have wished she had a job to go to that Monday to keep her occupied. She wished Emmy wasn't away; she needed her and her vague moments that called for her patient understanding. She needed something to keep her mind off Neve. She felt dreadful that for even a moment she had suspected him of being less than the man he was. She felt terrible that *before* she had telephoned him he had already given his personnel manager instructions to use the agency.

She had several spasms that day of going off into a dream world, of thinking how wonderful it would be if he loved her half as much as she loved him. But by the time she went to bed her dreams had been put away as hopeless fantasy. She would not be seeing him again. After Saturday he would never ask for her again. And maybe that was for the best. Cope with his work she could, but how could she hope to cope with seeing him, and hiding what was in her heart?

That week was one of the worst Darcy could remember. She felt bereft. When she had lost her parents Emmy had been there to help. Perhaps I'll feel better when she gets back, she thought disconsolately on Friday night.

Emmy arrived home on Saturday full of her holiday, declaring she had had a splendid time, but was glad to be home. Darcy hugged her and fussed round her, pleased to see she was looking so well, Emmy recounted many episodes on and off through the afternoon. She repeated the same tale several times, but she often did that, and Darcy listened patiently as though it was the first time she had heard it.

They were sharing a pot of tea, in a lull which let Neve into Darcy's mind, when Emmy suddenly said:

'I've done nothing but talk about me since I got back. Tell me about what you've been doing, dear.' And on top of that, 'How are you getting along with that nice Mr Macalister?'

Not ready for the question, Darcy glanced at the

beaming face waiting expectantly for an answer. Then, her brain going into action, she saw that with Emmy's mind being still on her holiday, she was going to grow confused if she didn't keep her reply simple.

'Fine,' she said. 'Just fine.' Then she knew Emmy was already confused when she said:

'Is it tomorrow we're going to his home?'

'Er——' began Darcy, caught unprepared again, glancing at Emmy and seeing she was now looking tired—she hadn't had so much as a catnap since she got off the coach. 'No, love,' she said, and settled for, 'Not tomorrow.' She would explain that she had already been to his home—and would not be going again—when Emmy had rested and would be less likely to be upset at her memory lapse that Darcy had gone to Neve's home on the same day she had gone to Brighton.

Emmy was in her bedroom unpacking when just after six the phone rang. Darcy answered the phone—and nearly dropped it. It was Neve.

Not expecting to hear from him again, just the sound of his voice had her insides churning. She had no single idea why he should ring, but she knew, because Jane had not asked her to do 'phone duty', that it couldn't be about work. It wasn't.

'I'm ringing to ask you to have dinner with me tonight.' Invitation it was, though his voice sounded gruff, and not very inviting at all as he came stright to the point.

But dinner with him? Oh no! Though she wanted with everything in her to say yes, folly only lay in that direction. 'No,' she replied. And because of what he had done, would do, for Jane, that 'No' sounded much too blunt, she added, 'Thank you, Neve, but I can't.'

She just hadn't expected him to argue either. But after a short pause, it sounded as if he was prepared to do just that, for to her surprise, she heard him ask:

'Why can't you?'

'I . . .' she began. What? Tell him she couldn't go out with him because she was in love with him? That if he kissed her again as he had the last time, told her as he had before that he wanted her, she didn't know that she wouldn't be giving in to him, but that it wasn't just one evening in his arms she wanted? 'A girl has a right to say no if—if she fancies,' she said, making her voice cold, wanting this conversation to finish, afraid of the weakness he wrought in her.

She thought she would be hearing a short sharp answer. Desire her he did, she knew that, just as she knew too that Neve wasn't a man likely to ask her a second time.

And then his voice came again, deliberate, making her colour flare, making her glad he couldn't see the way her hand came out and grabbed the table for support that he had no qualms when it came to being blunt.

'You fancied me once,' he reminded her.

From she knew not where, Darcy found, 'You—serve a fairly potent wine,' and showed she couldn't handle it, calling herself all sorts of an idiot afterwards, by quietly putting down the phone.

'Was that Jane, dear?' asked Emmy, coming into the room, a china ornament in her hand she had purchased in Brighton.

'No, love,' said Darcy, hiding her eyes from Emmy as she concentrated on the china dog. 'just a—a friend.'

On Sunday morning Emmy was a little off colour, but wouldn't stay in bed. 'It's probably the effect of travelling yesterday,' she said when Darcy suggested it wouldn't hurt her to have an extended lie-in. 'I'll take things easy today and be as right as ninepence tomorrow, you'll see.'

Darcy insisted she let her cook the Sunday lunch, and while Emmy dozed afterwards she washed and dried up, beginning to think she was looking a little better. So much so that when Jane rang to say she had a job for her that evening that had just come in, and that she should be back home by about eleven, she thought it would be all right to leave the old lady.

Thinking it must be a waitressing job—sitting with pregnant whippets didn't come in too often—she had every confidence that Jane wouldn't send her to work in another ghastly club, after her report about that last one. But caution came suddenly as the thought struck her that it might be a driving job. It held her back from saying she could do it, reminding her that she still hadn't told Jane about that disastrous delivery job in Banbury.

'What sort of job?' she asked.

'One with a difference, actually,' said Jane. 'That's to say, we've never had one like it before. But as our slogan says "Any job", when Mr Macalister . . .'

'Neve Macalister?' Oh, she had been right to be cautious!

'That's right. His firm have put another firm on to us, by the way. Anyway, to get back to the job; there's this Frenchman and his wife who flew in today—Mr Macalister is having business discussions or something with the Frenchman tomorrow—but for tonight he's entertaining them. The wife is nothing to do with the business, so he thought it would be nice if she had another woman to talk to. She doesn't speak English, but he said he knew you could speak French . . .'

'He asked for me?'

'Oh yes, didn't I say? He seems very impressed with your efficiency, Darcy. Wants you to meet them at the . . .'

Her talk went over Darcy's head. She hated letting the agency down, but knew by now that Neve wouldn't hold it against the agency. He had shown he was too much of a man for that. And anyway, aside from her French not being brilliant, she had a growing suspicion that it wouldn't be needed—that there was no French couple. Neve was being more persistent than she had thought he would be, but at the bottom of this lay the fact he still wanted her. And she had no need to convince herself that once he had assuaged his desire, there would be no room in his life for her. And suddenly she was angry—angry that he was so determined she should dine with him, and more—that he wasn't beyond going through the agency to get her.

'. . . so will you do it?' Jane was ending.

'I'm sorry,' she said, careful not to let Jane suspect her anger, 'but N . . . Mr Macalister must have got it all wrong. My French is terrible.' And, a lovely idea coming, 'Myra speaks French fluently, she's just the person.'

'I didn't know she spoke French!'

'Oh yes,' said Darcy, doubting Myra's French was any better than her own—still, she wouldn't be needing it.

'He did specially ask for you,' said Jane doubtfully. Then, the business woman in her taking over, 'Though if he wants someone to converse in French with the French lady, Myra would be better if, as you say, her French is fluent.' Darcy's smile started, broadened as she pictured Neve's face when Myra turned up. Then Jane was sending that smile speeding, as she remarked, 'And Myra isn't exactly repulsive-looking for him to mind her being a substitute, is she?'

She'd brought it on herself, Darcy thought as, both she and Emmy retiring early, she lay in bed trying to oust the picture of the far from repulsive, nay very attractive Myra, dining in a cosy twosome with Neve.

Jealousy had had her in its grip from the moment Jane had referred to Myra's looks. She would absolutely loathe and detest it if Neve used Myra as a substitute for her in any way to ease the desire he had for her. Myra made no secret that she wasn't averse to going to bed with a man if she fancied him. And who wouldn't fancy Neve when he asserted even a small amount of his charm!

After an awful night when she awakened every hour and wondered if Myra had gone home alone or was she still with Neve, Darcy got out of bed the next morning with that nagging jealousy still with her.

She selected the clothes she was to wear that day to go to the receptionist's job she had been assigned to, and was crossing the short hall to the bathroom when she heard Emmy coughing. And then all jealousy vanished and every other thought. Emmy very often coughed first thing in the morning, but that cough sounded different.

In seconds Darcy was in her room, her eyes quickly noting the bright colour in the otherwise faded cheeks of her beloved Emmy.

'Try to sit up, love,' she said, going over and propping her up with pillows.

'I'm all right,' the old lady wheezed. But she couldn't be feeling too bright, Darcy thought, since she made only a light protest when she told her she thought it might be as well to let the doctor have a look at her.

Having nursed Emmy through many bouts of illness, Darcy knew just what to do to make her comfortable. It wasn't urgent that Dr Ferguson came to see her straight away, past experience told Darcy that. She decided to wait until the surgery was open rather than put through an emergency call. Though she'd better get on to Jane without delay and give her time to get someone else to do the job she had been going to.

'You'd better count me out this week,' she told Jane after she had explained that today was definitely out.

'We're a bit busy,' Jane hinted, something that would have pleased Darcy at any other time.

'Well, it may only be a couple of days thing with Emmy. She's had short bouts before. She might be all right again by Thursday,' Darcy told her, keeping her fingers crossed for Emmy's sake. 'I'll let you know the moment I'm available.'

Darcy took another peep at Emmy who, though still wheezy, had finished coughing, then she went to wash and dress, discarding the smart outfit she would have worn, and slipping into jeans and a shirt.

As soon as she thought someone would be on duty at the surgery, she rang through, leaving a message for the doctor to call, then making sure Emmy was kept warm, she went to the sitting room and began tidying up.

On the stroke of nine the phone rang. Darcy answered

it without giving any mind to who was calling—and promptly had her ears blasted for her trouble.

'Where the hell were you last night?' roared Neve Macalister.

And jealousy was back with her, making void any speculation she might have had that he didn't sound as though his evening had been so successful, nullifying all thought that he must have phoned on the offchance she might be home and not out on a job. All she could think of was him—him and Myra.

'Didn't you get on well with Myra?'

She had wanted it to come out sweetly sarcastic, but was horrified to hear it sound as though she was longing for him to say that he hadn't.

He didn't answer straight away. In fact there was a very definite pause. Just as though he had suspected she was out of sorts because he had been out with another woman, and was speculating on the thought, she thought, feeling ill, not wanting him to have the smallest suspicion she had lost sleep on account of him.

His voice came again—and this time he wasn't roaring. 'You sound—jealous,' he said softly at last. And she hated him, hated his shrewdness—and was in there fast to deny it.

'Rubbish,' she said stoutly, but was prodded and poked at by that same emotion she was denying, and her voice was nowhere near as airy as she would have wished. 'Did the evening—er—go off all right?' And pulling herself together, 'I mean, the French . . .'

'I found Myra perfectly charming,' Neve drawled, adding, having Darcy feeling too much, not thinking at all, 'I do hope she isn't too exhausted to fulfil her other duties today. It was . . .'

Aghast, Darcy looked at the phone back on its rest, realising, unable to bear to hear any more, she had slammed it down. God she groaned, sinking on to the nearest chair. Neve had suspected she was jealous—she had just proved it. She hadn't been able to take it when he had indicated that he and Myra . . .

She was calmer, but still being torn apart by jealousy when a few minutes later the phone rang again. It wouldn't be Neve, she knew that. But it was. And never had she heard his voice more silky.

'I hadn't finished,' he drawled.

Darcy took a deep breath. She knew she had to send from his head any idea she was one iota bothered by anything he had got up to with Myra, and at last had the note she was looking for, her voice sounding careless, just as though she didn't give a hoot.

'Contrary to your belief,' she said offhandedly, 'I don't require a blow-by-blow account of . . .'

'You weren't going to get one.' He was straight away back to being the gritty, harsh-voiced man she was more familiar with. 'I rang, because I have a job for you.'

'You know the agency's number.'

'I'm ringing your number because I don't want a substitute.' What little comfort she gained from that was dashed when he added, 'You're a damn fine secretary. I need . . .'

'Mrs Knight has 'flu?' Pain kicked sarcasm into life—and Neve didn't like it.

'Her husband has,' he rapped.

'If you ring Mrs Davis I'm sure she'll find you someone . . .'

'Damn you, Darcy,' he roared, 'I want *you*!'

His tone ignited her wrath, the hurt in her ready to fling any ammunition she could lay her hands on. 'I recall you telling me that once before,' she flared. 'I told you then the agency doesn't . . .'

It was as far as she got. Neve had the upper hand, she discovered, and did not have time to waste bandying words, as his orders came brusque, sharp down the line.

'If you don't want me to withdraw my support from that agency, and advise my associates likewise,' he threatened, 'you'll be in my office within an hour of me putting this phone down!'

Darcy gasped at the hardness in him. He meant it! It

was there in his voice. He meant it, damn him—he wasn't playing games.

'I . . .' she began, her anger gone, 'I can't,' and knew he was going to put the phone down and straightway proceed to issue orders countermanding all other orders to his personnel manager. A brief phone call to any of his business associates, and they too would be ringing their personnel managers.

'Very well,' he said sternly.

'Neve,' she said quickly, and felt relief that she hadn't heard a click, that he was still there, when after ageless seconds she heard him bite the one word:

'Yes?'

'Neve,' she said again, knowing she had to tell him just why, in this instance, she couldn't work for him, 'I can't come to your office because—I can't leave home.'

A pause, 'Why?' Then the question was coming rapidly, 'You're not ill?'

'No, it's not me. It's Emmy—Miss Emsworth. She's poorly, chesty this morning, and I—can't leave her.'

Silence was her reply. And as it stretched, she just knew he wasn't believing her—had never believed there was any such person as Miss Emsworth. 'I'm expecting the doctor to call after his surgery,' she told him hurriedly, becoming desperate, thoughts of Jane and the agency crowding in as she gave him the doctor's telephone number, and told him, 'If you don't believe me, give Dr Ferguson a ring. He'll already have Miss Emsworth down on his call list. I phoned his surgery earlier.'

She felt beaten when Neve didn't answer. She had done her best, but having started off not trusting her an inch, Neve Macalister wasn't likely to believe her now. He knew of her loyalty to Jane, knew when Myra had gone in her place last night—she mustn't start thinking of that again—that she didn't want to see or work for him again. But since he didn't think there was any such person as Emmy, he would see what she had said about her being poorly as pure invention to get the agency off the hook. She didn't know just what else she could say to try and get him to see she was speaking the truth.

'Don't you think,' Neve broke his silence, his voice steady, 'with the old lady's chest dragging her down all the time, that it would be far better for her if she was living in the country?'

Was he believing her? 'You—do believe me?' she asked, a catch in her voice. 'You believe I do have Emmy living with me?'

Her answer was a bluntly asked, 'Are you lying?' And she heard what could have been a strangely tense note in his voice, as though he wanted to believe her—but heaven help her if she was stringing him along.

'No,' she choked, her hand gripping the phone. 'No, I'm not lying to you. I—did before, I admit, when I told you—at the beginning—that I lived alone. But I was afraid then you might send those men I thought were thugs to my home.' She had long since realised they were the security men he had said they were, top security men who were on his payroll. 'I—didn't want Emmy frightened.'

A long pause followed, then his voice came again, with a controlled evenness as decisively he did away with the reason for his call.

'It seems I shall have to rustle up a secretary from somewhere else, then, won't I?'

And then her eyes were brimming that at last, at last he believed her. He must do to be accepting her reason why she could not work for him as valid, he was returning to the subject of Emmy and her frail chest, and saying:

'But to get back to the old dear, don't you think it would be better for her to live away from London?'

'Er—yes, of course it would,' she agreed, her tears drying as she wondered which tack he was on now. 'But I simply can't afford . . .' and was smartly interrupted.

'I can.'

For several numbed moments Darcy wasn't with him. Then what was behind his remark hit her, and she was winded. She was gasping that what he must be saying was that he still wanted her, and that . . .

'You mean . . .' she choked, her mind reeling. Surely he couldn't be blatantly suggesting what she thought he was suggesting. 'You're—offering us both a home?'

'I never meant to discuss this over the phone,' he replied. 'I'll come . . .'

'Are you?' Her voice was taut, tense. She didn't relax when she heard his exasperated, aggressive answer.

'What the hell do you think I'm doing chasing you if that's not what I mean?'

All the answer she could want was there. But with what he had said knocking her sideways, even with his aggression to the fore, Darcy still persisted. When she put the phone down, she didn't want there to be any mistake.

'Are you?' she asked quietly. 'Are you offering Emmy and me a home with . . .'

'Damn you, yes!' he roared, not waiting for her to finish. And, the roar vanishing, 'But it's a good deal more than that . . .'

And Darcy, not letting him finish this time, knew full well exactly what the 'good deal more' implied.

'Don't ring me, I'll ring you,' she said with finality, and quietly put down the phone.

She spent two minutes lost in useless tears at his offering her a 'good deal more than that'. Neve would be more than generous, instinctively she knew that. But, did he think she would be his for a few trinkets? And what did he think Emmy and she would do once he had grown tired of her? Move back to London? Start flat-hunting again? Return to Adaptable Temps?

When the phone went again she somehow knew, even though she had been certain no one put the phone down on him twice, that it would be Neve.

'I don't think you properly understood, Darcy,' he said. But she had understood all right, and wasted no time in hanging up on him.

She went in to see Emmy knowing full well why she hadn't stayed to hear Neve out. She was afraid—afraid of herself and that weakness in her. She was afraid, wanting some time with him, however brief, that she might listen to him. And she couldn't listen to him. There wasn't only herself to think about. She had Emmy and her welfare to consider in everything she did.

Because Emmy liked to look out into the street when she was confined to her bed, she had the bedroom in front. And it was when Darcy, not long returned from getting the prescription filled that Dr Ferguson had given her—his opinion that Emmy's attack was a mild one, and that she would be over it in a couple of days, had been a great relief—that as she was recapping the bottle after administering the first dose, she heard the front door bell go. Setting the bottle down on Emmy's bedside table, Darcy glanced out of the window, then froze.

She knew that car parked out there, that Mercedes parked next to hers, just as the caller, who knew her car, would know she was in. Hastily she came away from the window.

'Was that the door, dear?'

'It's—er—I think it's somebody selling something,' said Darcy, hoping Emmy wouldn't turn to study Neve when no one answered and he went back to his car. He just didn't look like anybody's idea of a door-to-door salesman.

The bell went again. 'Do you think you should go and answer it?' Emmy suggested.

'We don't need anything,' Darcy told her, praying Neve would go away. Put down the phone on him she could, but tell him to his face she never wanted to see him again would be beyond her. She mustn't be weak and let him in—she mustn't. She had Emmy to think of.

She wouldn't have been surprised if he'd started banging on the woodwork. But when he didn't, she was so full of love for him that that streak of kindness in him must have extended to him not wanting to scare her eighty-two-year-old, at present invalid companion, out of her wits, Darcy almost went to answer the door.

She looked at Emmy then, frail and worn in her all-enveloping flannel nightdress, and the impulse was gone.

Neve rang the bell just once more. Then Darcy heard his footsteps and wanted desperately to look out of the window. She wanted one last glimpse of him, but dare not look out until she heard his car start up.

An early visit to Emmy's room the next morning showed that the medication taken at regular intervals yesterday had done its work well.

'I think I'll get up today,' she said perkily, looking so much better, and declaring there wasn't a thing wrong with her.

'I wanted to give the sitting room a springclean this morning,' said Darcy guilelessly. 'You wouldn't like to stay in bed until after lunch, would you?'

'Of course, dear,' said Emmy amiably.

When at half past ten that morning the phone rang, Darcy answered it fearfully. Had she known it would be Neve, she would not have answered it at all.

'Don't hang up,' were his first words.

She resisted the impulse, though she asked, none too politely, 'Well?'

'I want to talk to you, but not over the phone,' he said shortly. 'Will you open the door today if I come round?'

He wasn't under any illusion about yesterday when he had called then! 'There's nothing you can say that I want to hear,' she said stubbornly.

'You're saying you won't open the door?' Aggression was beginning to bite.

'Got it in one!' she snapped, and heard him let go with that aggression. She was numbed by it, so that she was still holding on to the phone.

'You obstinate bitch!' he hurled down the wires. 'Well, hear this, Darcy Alexander, and hear it good. You are *going* to see me, *going* to hear me out whether you want to or not—I'll get to you one way or another!'

Darcy was still holding on to the instrument, too

stunned by what she had heard to make any reply. But this time it wouldn't have mattered what she said. Neve wasn't there. He had done what he had told her not to do. He had hung up.

CHAPTER TEN

HAVING spent the rest of Tuesday, at the very least from the tone Neve had used expecting at any moment to have the front door come crashing in, his foot against it, Darcy went to bed that night still wary of his threat, even though she had seen nothing of him.

On Wednesday Emmy was so much better that when it was time to go to bed, Darcy thought tomorrow she could safely ring Jane to see if she had any work for her.

Of Neve she had seen neither hide nor hair, and she lay in bed more puzzled than wary—and if she were to be honest, a shade disappointed. Of course she hadn't the slightest intention of falling in with his bright idea that she and Emmy move into his home for a while, but life was dull, flat, without hearing from him. And she just couldn't understand either, when there had been a most definite threat in what he had said, that he had not followed through his sworn, 'You are *going* to see me, whether you want to or not!'

Dr Ferguson called again on Thursday morning, gave Emmy a going over in the sitting room, since she refused to stay in bed, and proclaimed she was over her attack and that there was no need for him to call again. He seemed grateful for Darcy's offer of coffee, saying he'd got just time enough for a quick cup, and stayed chatting to Emmy while Darcy dashed into the kitchen to make it.

Coming back with the coffee tray, she was just in time to hear Emmy stating her belief, 'I shall be visiting the country for the weekend soon,' and puckishly, 'That will do me far more good than all your medicines.'

'You could well be right,' he agreed, going along with

the elderly lady. And with the doctor there, it just wasn't the moment when Darcy could contradict her and gently tell her she had got it all wrong.

With Dr Ferguson giving Emmy a clear bill of health, Darcy rang Jane as soon as he had gone, and what she learned from her friend and employer, sent from her mind any resolve that after her phone call she was going to have a few carefully tactful words with Emmy on the subject of her *not* going to the country for a weekend.

'Emmy's fine again now,' she told Jane, while Emmy, comfortably out of earshot, was washing up the coffee things in the kitchen. 'Any work for me?'

Jane sounded relieved to hear her. 'I've accepted a job for tomorrow, so I'm glad you've phoned. I particularly wanted you for it . . .)'

'It's not for Neve Macalister, is it?' Darcy asked quickly, nervously. Had he particularly asked for her? Was this his way of making sure she saw him? 'I don't . . .' she began in a rush.

'Relax,' said Jane, a touch of humour in her voice. 'It's not with Macalister Precision Equipment. Though if you've something against Mr Macalister it beats me what it is. He was perfectly charming when he phoned to ask if you were working this week.'

'*He* phoned you?' Darcy's head was starting to spin.

'Yes,' Jane confirmed. 'I felt rather flattered, actually. It's usually his personnel manager I speak with. But Mr Macalister himself phoned yesterday to thank me for sending Myra along.' Vivid green darts of jealousy stabbed at Darcy while Jane went on, 'It was just a courtesy call really, I suppose, though he did go on to hope—since he'd asked for you by name for that French job, I expect—to hope you weren't ill or anything.' He knew damn well she wasn't ill, Darcy thought, beginning to wonder what his angle was. 'So then I explained about Miss Emsworth being off colour . . .'

'You told him about Emmy?' Darcy exclaimed, though not for the reason Jane obviously thought.

'Well, I didn't think you'd mind,' said her friend, a frown in her voice. 'You don't, do you, Darcy? I mean, he's a very important client, and—and well, it doesn't hurt to give a bit in business. And he must think a lot of your abilities, because he asked me to let him know the moment you were ready to work again.'

Darcy came away from the phone with the details of the job she was to do tomorrow written down on her notepad, her heart crying out in pain.

She no longer believed in Neve Macalister's threat to make her see and hear him. His telling Jane he wanted to know when she was available for work was so much flannel, a way, having got the information he wanted from Jane, of charmingly terminating the conversation.

Very clearly she saw just why he had personally phoned Jane. His purpose was to check the truth with her that there really was an elderly lady called Miss Emsworth as she had told him. He had phoned the agency to check that she really did live with Emmy— and she had thought he had trusted her, that he had believed her!

Emmy coming into the room asking, 'Did Jane have a job for you, dear?' took her mind temporarily away from the distrustful Neve Macalister.

'For tomorrow afternoon,' she said, forcing a smile. And consulting her notepad, was glad she had taken down what Jane had said, for the state her mind was in she would never have remembered it. 'I hope it's as easy as it sounds. I have to sit beside a lady who's just passed her driving test after the fourteenth attempt, but who feels nervous driving on her own.'

Darcy refrained from telling her what else she had written in her shorthand, that the newly qualified driver was a lady of more mature years, and that was why Jane thought she would be particularly suitable for the job, as she was so patient with elderly people. But on checking through the details, she saw she had forgotten to get the woman's address.

There being no special hurry to get the address, Darcy left it until after lunch to ring Jane, taking down the address she thought might take her three-quarters of an hour to get to depending on traffic. Then instead of saying cheerio to Jane, she just could not hold back on the urge to know . . .

'I—er—don't suppose you've been in touch with Mr Macalister—er—to tell him I'm back in business, have you?'

'I have, as a matter of fact—well, I promised him I would.' And when Darcy had already decided Neve Macalister would not be asking her to work for him again, she promptly felt piqued when Jane went on, 'I told him you had a job that would keep you fully occupied tomorrow afternoon, expecting him to say "Can we have her from Monday?" but I must have caught him at a busy moment, because after thanking me politely, he said nothing more—just hung up.'

He was good at hanging up, Darcy thought sourly, forgetting she wasn't too bad at it herself. So it was over, finished. He had grown tired of chasing her. She sniffed, and thought if she had any sense, she should be glad.

Her job sitting beside the prim Miss Pringle the following afternoon left no room for her to dwell on Neve Macalister and his being the cause of her insomnia. Though she did wonder briefly, when Miss Pringle applied the brakes with such force she nearly hit the windscreen, if Neve would send flowers if Miss Pringle didn't get them back to base in one piece.

'Wasn't so bad, was it?' questioned Miss Pringle boisterously, despite her sixty-eight years. 'I'll ring the agency the next time I feel like a spin.' And as if she was doing her a favour, 'I'll ask for you, Miss Alexander.'

Darcy drove herself home wanting nothing more than a strong cup of tea laced with plenty of sugar, wishing she hadn't held back on the temptation to tell Miss Pringle what an excellent driver Myra was.

Letting herself into her flat, she called, 'Emmy, it's me,' the way she always did. But today she received no reply. Thinking Emmy must be having a doze, she checked the sitting room, but found no Emmy napping in her favourite chair. Darcy looked into the kitchen without success, but it wasn't until she was going along the hall to Emmy's room that the first feelings of apprehension made themselves felt. 'Emmy!' she called again, but there was still no reply.

Emmy's bedroom door stood open, and, sure she must have heard her—if she was able to hear at all—Darcy was afraid of what she might find, and had to take a second out to get a grip on herself before she went in.

There was no Emmy there. Darcy's tension did not relax as her brow puckered. Emmy would have gone along to her club this afternoon, but she was always home by four-thirty, and it was now a quarter to six!

Having checked the bathroom and her own bedroom with no sign of her, beset with fear, Darcy hurried to the sitting room, and was approaching the phone about to ring Mrs Bricknell when she spotted the note propped up against it.

Relief that Emmy had thought to leave a note before she had trotted off somewhere didn't have time to get started, as she snatched up the note, and her eyes grew wider and wider. Even before she read it she knew she had seen that writing somewhere before—and it wasn't Emmy's writing.

But she would know that writing anywhere. The last time she had seen that particular hand had been when she was working for Neve Macalister! What on earth had he been doing in their flat? And where the dickens was Emmy?

Quickly scanning what Neve had penned, Darcy soon had the answer to both questions. And she had never been more furious in her life.

'The *swine!* The *bastard*!' she muttered, enraged, as she raced out to her car. How dared he do this to her?

The car shot forward as she crashed the gears and took off in a manner Miss Pringle would have thought of as normal, the line Neve had written flashing before her eyes, 'Now will you talk?' He had signed it 'N.'

She neither knew nor cared what sort of remark Neve Macalister would have made on her 'reprehensible driving' had he seen her as she put her foot down and headed for Cornthorpe. What she did know was that her supposition that he had grown tired of chasing her had been completely erroneous. He hadn't let up his pursuit of her, that was clear. Clear also was the fact that when he had called her an obstinate bitch and threatened 'I'll get to you one way or another' he had meant it.

And he thought by kidnapping Emmy he could force her to go to bed with him! Well, did he have another think coming! If he had so much as harmed one hair of Emmy's head, she'd kill him! How *could* he take advantage of Emmy's memory lapses? Emmy, dear soul, had been expecting to go to his home. She had probably told him so the minute he had told her who he was!

That some of the blame had to be hers that she hadn't put her right on that score, didn't help to lessen her anger. Guilt with herself fuelled it. How was she to know he would call at her home while she was out and make off with Emmy!

By the time she had left the main road and was driving round the winding lanes to Cornthorpe, Darcy had it all worked out. She knew exactly why Neve Macalister had phoned Jane showing an interest in her movements. It meant, of course, that he *had* believed her, had believed there was such a person as Emmy. Her fury with him wavered. That was until she realised he had planned this, the ruthless swine—planned it, right from the moment he had hung up, leaving her with his threat to think about. Planned, and waited his chance for her to leave the flat for a few hours—and then he had pounced.

With a squeal of tyres on gravel, Darcy announced her

arrival as she rammed on the brakes outside the large house where she was convinced Emmy had been taken. In a flash she was up the stone steps, too blindingly angry to think of ringing the door bell as with the flat of her hands she banged on the front door.

She heard someone coming and had no idea how she was going to be civil to Mrs Gow if it was the housekeeper who answered the racket she was kicking up.

It was not Mrs Gow who opened the door. Neve Macalister stood there, dark, cool, and casual. And Darcy swallowed. Her anger with him had had her putting aside how deeply she loved him. But that love for him hit her again, had her unspeaking, allowing him to get the first word in, as slowly, he drawled,

'I thought it might be you.'

It was his casual tone that got to her, sending weakness on its way. He had kidnapped her Emmy, and there didn't look to be an atom of guilt in him for what he had done. Without waiting to be invited, she was pushing past him, was over his threshold and turning in the wide hall to demand:

'Where's Emmy?'

He did not answer her straight away. Calmly ignoring that she looked ready to blow a fuse, he took hold of her arm, refusing to let go when she tried to shrug his hand away, and firmly he ushered her resisting form into the drawing room.

'Where is she?' Darcy snapped, and giving another tug, found she was free, that he had let go of her.

Or was she free? Neve had closed the door and was standing in front of it, immovable, by the look of it. Darcy saw then that there was no way she was going to get from the room without a fight.

'I demand to see Miss Emsworth,' she told him coldly, not liking at all the glint in those piercing dark eyes that said she was seeing no one until he had had that talk with her he had been after. She was unnerved, and she knew why. Over the phone she had been able to tell him she wasn't interested in his proposition. Face to face, her love for him undeniable, it was entirely another matter.

'I'll allow you to see Miss Emsworth presently,' said Neve coolly. 'Meantime . . .'

'Meantime nothing,' Darcy said hurriedly, desperately afraid she would fall apart if he so much as touched her again. Her own weakness fired anger, anger with herself that she might end up giving into him. 'How dare you go around kidnapping old ladies?' she challenged heatedly. 'The poor dear must have been frightened to death!'

'From where I'm standing,' he inserted smoothly, 'you, Darcy, appear to me to be far more frightened than the old dear ever was.'

She didn't want this to turn into a discussion about her. She forbore to swallow. Those shrewd eyes were not missing a thing. 'Where is Emmy?' she demanded again, though this time more to get his thoughts off her and how she appeared to him.

'She's quite safe,' said Neve, and smiled. 'Blair likes old people. Between them he and Mrs Gow are seeing that she's well looked after.'

'She'll want to see me,' said Darcy, eyeing the door, but afraid to go anywhere near it. Neve looked casual, but she didn't trust him not to take hold of her as he had that time before, if she went anywhere near that door.

'Stop worrying about her. She was quite happy to come with me.' He paused, his eyes fixing hers so she couldn't look away. 'In fact,' he said easily, 'she seemed to be expecting me to call.' Another pause, then, 'So much so that I had to wait only while she put on her coat and hat—she already had a weekend case packed.'

Darcy coloured, when she had done nothing to colour at. Neve always had been suspicious of her, he would never understand that she hadn't known herself that Emmy, anticipating a weekend away, had at some time packed ready for it.

'I didn't—tell her we—she was spending a weekend

here,' she said. Then her anger faded as she corrected herself, and went red again, 'Well, I did, but that was—the other time. The time she went to Brighton.'

'I know,' he said. And while Darcy looked at him in amazement to see that there wasn't a glimmer of suspicion about him, he added gently, 'You told me once she sometimes gets confused.' She felt better all of a sudden. That was until he said, 'That was borne out by one or two things she said on the way here.'

And Darcy, vulnerable where he was concerned, was hurt again that he *would* have been suspicious of her had not Emmy said something that had struck him as odd on the journey. 'Anyway,' she said, stronger now, nothing would induce her to stay in this house with a man who was still suspicious of her, 'you had no right to take her away. I told you myself she's been ill—or didn't you believe that either?'

'Of course I believed you,' he retorted, and astonishment was hers again that he could stand there and sound as if there had never been a time when he had thought her capable of lying. 'That's precisely why I first telephoned Dr Ferguson . . .'

'To check I was telling the truth,' she spurted in, hurt again.

'To see if she was well enough to travel,' he rapped back, getting angry where she was gaping. 'He assured me the journey would do her no harm at all.'

Darcy quickly overcame her feelings. Neve seemed to think he had the upper hand again, and it was up to her to show him he hadn't.

'Good,' she snapped. 'In that case it won't harm her at all that I'm taking her straight back.'

Exasperated suddenly, Neve looked ready to lose his temper with her completely. He knew anyway, she thought, that he was wasting his time trying to have that talk he wanted with her. Then she saw he had controlled whatever he was feeling, as tightly he told her:

'By removing Miss Emsworth from your home I've made her my responsibility. I am *not* having you driving

her back to London at this time of night, when the night
air can have nothing but a harmful effect on her bron-
chial condition.'

And before Darcy could get in there and tell him
Emmy was her responsibility and no one else's, he was
saying:

'I've had the room you used last time prepared for
you,' and by his look striving to remember he was host,
he tacked on as amiably as his tethered anger would
allow, 'Perhaps you would like to go up to your room
until dinner. We can get down to the discussion we
should have had a week ago when dinner has put you in
a better frame of mind.'

He moved from the door, and the way from the room
was unguarded. Darcy knew then he had no mind to
prevent her leaving. If her ears had heard right he was
suddenly fed up with her, and was *ordering* her from the
room.

But she made no move to go. Anger that had been
stunned by the controlled fury of him roared into life at
his icy assumption that he could order her about—he
wasn't, via Adaptable Temps, her employer this trip.
And never, she thought, furious at his lofty attitude,
would she ever be in a better frame of mind than right
now to have *that* discussion.

'If you still have it in your mind to ask me to come
and live here with you,' she told him, mad enough not
to dress up what she knew all this was about, 'then you
can just jolly well forget it!' Neve's brow came down—
he wasn't liking what he was hearing, she could see that.
But fury wouldn't keep her tongue quiet, for all it had
started to falter. 'You might as well know now, N-Neve
Macalister, that I have no intention n-now or at any
time of ever becoming your m-mistress,' she ended.

And then had never felt so dreadful in her life as his
expression changed, and that look appeared that told
her she had got hold of the wrong end of the stick.

Oh God! she thought, going scarlet with mortifica-
tion, more confused than Emmy had ever been. Just

because he had desired her, told her he wanted her, she had taken it on herself to assume ... She gulped on her embarrassment. She had assumed what she had when she knew full well he was a workoholic, when she had personal knowledge that he was capable of producing sufficient work for two secretaries. He had said more than once that she was a good secretary.

She hurried to the door, unable to look at him. Work was all that mattered to him. Because of her need for him she had not looked beyond her *own* need, had thought ... When all the time all he had wanted was someone to clear up the work he did in the evenings and at weekends.

'I'm—sorry,' she choked, her hand reaching blindly for the door handle. 'I g-got it all wrong, didn't I?'

She wasn't intending to stay and hear his answer. But the hand that shot out and grasped her wrist before she could turn the door handle, the hand that turned her back into the room, was telling her that now they had got started, Neve was insisting on finishing it out.

'I'm sorry,' she said again, refusing to look at him. She would never be able to look him in the face again, she thought. 'You want a home-based secretary, don't you? I—I should have seen that b-before.'

The hold on her wrist intensified, but Darcy was in too much mental agony to feel physical pain. Then Neve was heaping fresh confusion on her by suddenly letting go her wrist and grating:

'Excellent secretary you are,' not making it sound like a compliment. 'But do you really believe I would go so far as to remove Miss Emsworth from your home just because I want a home-based secretary?' And while her mouth went dry—she just hadn't got to thinking that far—he was biting into her, 'After the way we react to each other you think I want you in my home just to decorate my study?'

'I—you ...' Her head shot up, her eyes going to his steady all-seeing stare, and away again. 'You mean—I was—er ...' Her nerves were showing. She felt she had already made too much of a fool of herself. But—but what else could he be meaning but . . .

'I mean I want you in my home, period,' he told her, his voice cold—or was it just that he was being so very deadly serious? Darcy admitted she was mixed up. 'I want you decorating every room in my home, this room, the dining room, my—bedroom.'

Colour flared again. There was no mistaking his meaning this time. Had she not felt so weak, Darcy was sure she would have hit him.

'This is where I came in,' she said stiffly, and anger came to assist her. 'I have no intention of decorating so much as one room in your home a minute longer than I have to. As soon as I can find Emmy, I'm leaving.'

'I haven't finished yet.' His aggression was out in the open, but she had heard more than enough.

She made to turn to the door, and was made angrier to feel his hand on her wrist again. Didn't he know he was tearing her to shreds? Didn't he know the fight she was having not to give in? Didn't he have any idea that she loved him so much she was in danger of throwing in her lot with him regardless of how she and Emmy would fare afterwards? That reminder of Emmy gave her the strength she needed.

'*I've* finished,' she said bluntly. 'We have nothing more to discuss.' And her voice rose, panic hitting her that if he didn't soon take his hand from her wrist, she would go under, already she felt she was drowning. 'And take your hand off me! I want to find Emmy. I am *not* going to be y-your mistress—and—and that's all there is to it!'

For answer, Neve's other hand came and grasped her other wrist. He had her securely manacled, and had turned her so she could see into his eyes—if she'd had a mind to look up, which she didn't.

That was until, his voice level, he said something that startled her so much her head jerked up in astonishment.

'How would you react to being my mistress if I put a

wedding ring on your finger?'

Too witless then to read anything in those dark eyes except that it definitely wasn't anger she saw there, Darcy stared at him in utter stupefaction. She saw the smile that started to break at the corners of his mouth at her shattered look, and tried, not believing she had heard what she thought she had heard, to try and get her scattered wits together.

'A—a real w-wedding ring?' she stammered.

'A real wedding ring,' he confirmed, his smile fading.

Darcy cleared her throat with a small coughing sound. 'W-with a—a certificate to—to prove it?'

There wasn't a smile about him then. His face was stern, serious. 'With a marriage certificate to prove it,' he said, and looked steadily, piercingly, into her eyes as though trying to read her answer there.

But Darcy, more confused then ever, stunned, did not want him reading anything. She lowered her eyes, concentrating her attention on the vee of the navy sweater he had on over his blue open-necked shirt. Why? she was asking herself. Why? She couldn't believe Neve had actually asked her to marry him, but surely that was what, just a few seconds ago, he had done.

Was he still out to make her pay for being, as he thought, Stoddart's accomplice? It had to be that. Neve wasn't interested in marriage. His own brother had told her so.

'I thought you had a down on women who would do anything for money,' she said, having no intention of saying yes, she would marry him, only to find it was some macabre sort of joke he was playing for his own satisfaction.

'You wouldn't marry me for my money, Darcy Alexander,' he said, sounding positive, 'I know that.' Amazed he sounded so certain, she looked up and found his eyes were still fastened on her. 'Had you been interested in a man with a fat bank balance you would have married one long ago,' he continued to amaze her by adding.

Darcy gave herself a mental shake. She hadn't a clue what all this was about, but it was more than about time she asserted herself. 'Do I say a grateful thanks for your high opinion of me?' she asked, and saw at once from the narrowing of his eyes that he didn't appreciate her sarcasm.

But he didn't rise to it as matter-of-factly he told her, 'You could have any man you chose, and you know it.'

Dumbfounded, she saw he actually believed that! And her heart, that hadn't been exactly steady, started beating a wayward rhythm over which she had no control. She opened her mouth, but discovered she was too taken aback by what must be a compliment, to find anything to say, then heard a tough note enter Neve's voice as, not waiting for her to get vocal release, he said grittily:

'Only I just couldn't allow that . . .'

'Couldn't allow . . .' she interrupted, making an effort, her voice fading when Neve let go her wrists and his hands came to her shoulders, this time in the most gentle of holds.

'I couldn't allow you to marry any man but me, Darcy Alexander.'

She cleared her throat. 'You sound as though you—er—think I might—er—want to marry you,' she managed, wishing her voice was stronger.

'I've been a swine to you, I know it,' he said gruffly, and his voice didn't sound much stronger than hers as he admitted, 'But who knows what I shall do if you won't marry me.' Never more serious, his voice more on even keel, he gently shook her, then said, 'You've rubbed my nose in the dirt for long enough, girl.' Then he took a deep breath, and revealed, 'I don't think I can take any more.'

Darcy had never consciously rubbed anyone's nose in the dirt, had never had any idea that was what Neve had felt when she had run from his chasing.

'But I . . .' she began to protest.

Then suddenly it occurred to her that if by running from him she had hurt him—as she had been hurt—

then she could not bear that he should be hurt any more. It came to her that she should stop running and try to believe in this moment, in the way, if she was right—Neve had grown to believe in her.

'You—want me so badly?' she asked chokily.

'Yes, I do,' he nodded, not dressing it up—it wasn't his way.

'So badly you'll marry me to . . .'

His hands gripping her shoulders stopped her from finishing. But she was so totally haywire, she wasn't sure what she had been going to say anyway, other than that this just had to have something to do with Neve wanting to possess her—but yet—he didn't believe in marriage for himself.

'As badly as that,' he said, refusing to let her continue with what she had started. 'The plain truth, my dear, is that I've done something I never thought I would. I've fallen in love. With you.'

Instinct had her trying to pull away. She had never suspected he might love her—it couldn't be true! Surely she was going to wake up and find this was just another punishment for the blackmailing tendencies he thought she possessed.

'Please don't,' she cried, finding it wasn't so easy to pull out of his hold. And pain filled her as she groaned, 'Haven't you punished me enough?'

She was in his arms, the agony in her voice too much. Neve held her to him, his voice crooning softly as he rocked her.

'My darling, have you any idea of how I break out in a cold sweat every time I think of the way I've been to you? When I think of the goodness I discovered in you, the truth in you I couldn't believe in—I just don't know how the hell I've got the nerve to ask you to forgive, to ask you to be my wife.'

He had her. He knew he had her. And Darcy, hearing that same pain in him she too had suffered, wanted to believe, had to believe, that he meant it when he said he loved her.

'C-could it be that—that you think I c-care for you?' she asked hesitantly.

He pulled back to look into her eyes. 'Not as deeply as I care for you.' Never had she heard that thrilling note of tenderness for her. 'But logic told me there had to be some reason why you were so afraid to see me.' She saw him swallow, heard the strain in him, as he asked, 'Did I delude myself totally that I heard jealousy in your voice when I told you I found Myra a very good substitute?'

That same jealousy had her going rigid. 'You say— you love me,' she said, icing up inside, nothing she could do to prevent that jealousy from rearing, 'and yet—yet you went to bed with her.'

'You *are* jealous!'

The pleased tone of his exclamation had her wrenching out of his arms, her expression tense. 'Yes, I am,' she admitted flatly, then found a yard away from him wasn't where Neve wanted her.

She was hauled back into his arms, and it seemed enough for him then just to hold her close, to murmur, 'My darling, my darling!'

'Did you go to bed with her?' It was no longer a statement, but a question—a question she just had to have the answer to, no matter how painful.

'I didn't even dine with her,' Neve whispered in her ear. 'When she arrived instead of you, we didn't get past the introduction stage—I packed her off in a taxi.'

'Oh, Neve!' The relief was heartfelt. Darcy felt the sting of tears. All her fretting about him and Myra had been for nothing!

She stayed with her head resting against his chest, content just to be there. She could hear the loud pounding of his heart and was amazed again that it was she who was making his heart act that way. Then she felt his hand come to the side of her face, lifting her head from his chest as he looked into her eyes and asked, needing to know the answer she had not yet given him:

'Marry me, Darcy?'

Her smile broke, lit her eyes, and she did nothing to hide it. 'Can I, please?' she asked—and had to know how much her answer meant to him when she felt the shudder of relief that went through him the moment before his head came down and he placed a warm kiss to the side of her mouth.

His face was only a fraction from hers when he asked, 'Will you try to love me a little, too?'

Her smile was there again. It stayed there in spite of the shyness in her that coloured her face pink as she told him, 'I—I've tried so hard to stop loving you ever since I knew what had happened to me the last time I was here.'

Neve Macalister was a man who never had any doubts about anything, she knew that. But as a muscle moved in his temple, she couldn't help seeing that at that moment he was looking strangely unsure, as he asked:

'You're saying—you love me?'

'Is that so incredible?'

'Yes. Oh, yes!'

And as his hold on her tightened, it seemed he could no longer resist the sweet invitation of her mouth. His lips met hers and for long delirious moments he kissed her. Ready to melt, Darcy wasn't too sure what he meant, when he broke their kiss and demanded:

'Tell me.'

'I love you,' she said, her heart bursting—and knew it was the right answer, when he again claimed her mouth and held her as though he would never let her go. Whispering endearments in her ear as he kissed her ears, kissed her eyes, her throat, her mouth, he finally half led, half carried her to a chair where he sat with her in his arms, and kissed her again, minutes passing before he pulled back.

And then it was to ask, a shadow of that alien uncertainty still about him, as having eyes for nowhere but her face, he asked, 'You won't run out on me again, Darcy, will you?'

'Never,' she replied promptly. And, shyly teasing,

'Though you didn't expect me to stay the last time, did you?'

'I did, my sweet love,' he confessed, planting a gentle kiss on her mouth. 'I actually did. I was staggered to find you gone. I didn't give thought that you might not stay the night.'

'You discovered I'd gone when I didn't come down to start work?'

'Before that,' he owned, a grin she found fascinating showing. 'Early on Sunday morning I went and made a pot of tea, laid a tray, pinched one of the roses from Mrs Gow's flower arrangement, popped it into a vase, and at six o'clock—I'd had one hell of a night—I brought it all up to your room.'

'You didn't?' Darcy gasped.

He smiled all the confirmation she could want. 'After you'd bolted from the drawing room I went to my study—I needed to think. I decided to ask you to marry me while you were still defenceless from sleep. To get your promise to be my wife before you had time to put your guard up.'

Darcy's face showed she was astounded. He had been planning to ask her to marry him while she had been weeping her way through that same 'hell of a night' he had spent!

'I'll stop at nothing to get you,' he told her, seeing he had rendered her speechless, not an ounce of shame in him.

'You—loved me then!'

'I began falling in love with you from the moment I saw you,' he confessed. 'But I just didn't want to admit what was happening even when I was reviling myself for being the cause of you having needed the attention of a doctor.'

He looked so grim at the memory that she just had to come in and help him out. 'You didn't know then that I wasn't up to my eyes in Stoddart's scheme.'

'I *should* have known,' he said firmly. 'There was nothing but innocence in you when you opened your eyes. Nothing there but such total innocence, all I wanted to do was to come over to where you lay, to protect you, to assure you that everything was all right.'

'But you didn't.'

'I didn't trust that emotion called love. Even while making you stay, not wanting to let you go, I didn't believe in love. I hardened my heart to the appeal of you, made myself think of Cordelia, of how you *had* to be instrumental in trying to ruin her marriage.'

'So it *was* Cordelia who was being blackmailed?' she asked on impulse, then straight away apologised, 'I'm sorry, I didn't mean to pry.'

'Anything that concerns my family concerns you,' Neve told her, as gently he kissed her.

Then he proceeded to show her just how much he trusted her, by revealing what Cordelia had told him.

'Before Cordelia met James Cunliffe, her husband, she became infatuated with Stoddart—became pregnant by him,' and while Darcy was getting over her surprise at hearing that, he went on, 'I was out of the country a good deal that year, and knew nothing of it until she came to me in panic in case James found out.'

'Stoddart was threatening to tell her husband about the child?' she guessed, wanting to do anything to take that stern look she had hoped never to see again from Neve's face.

'She miscarried,' he said briefly. 'But, obviously sedated, she wrote Stoddart a mixed-up letter from the hospital to the effect that her pregnancy had been aborted.'

'Oh!' Darcy exclaimed. And remembering, 'James Cunliffe spoke out strongly against abortion recently, didn't he?'

'So too did Cordelia,' Neve nodded. 'You can imagine her terror when she received a photostat of that letter purporting to have come from someone who said they'd found it. She showed it to me. It clearly indicated that she'd had an abortion. She was nearly demented at the laughing stock she thought the press would make of her husband if they got hold of it. I told her to tell James, but . . .'

'She loves her husband?'

'Very much. She said she couldn't tell him—yet she couldn't just ignore the demand for twenty thousand pounds.' He broke off when he saw how solemn Darcy was looking, and suddenly that stern expression had gone from him, as tenderly he smiled, and touched her cheek. 'I told her to leave it with me,' he ended.

Darcy smiled back. 'You went to see Stoddart?'

'I went to leave the money. Then I waited to see who collected it.' His look was apologetic. 'I had no idea, when I arranged for the deliverer of the letter to be brought to me, that Stoddart would use an agency—And he wasn't in any condition to tell me.'

'I hope you hit him hard,' said Darcy stoutly.

'I think you could say that,' Neve smiled again. Then, looking lovingly down at her, 'And I also think that's enough about Cordelia.'

Darcy's heart was in her smile, but she just had to ask, 'Why did you ask her to come to the office that first day I worked for you?'

Neve's hand, tender on her face, was a caress. 'Forgive me, my darling. I couldn't get you out of my head, yet I still didn't trust you. I had to have you working for me for the simple reason that I needed to see you. I watched you that morning going slowly out of my mind. When you went to lunch I phoned Cordelia, grasping at straws, hoping to gauge from your face when she arrived if there was more there than just plain recognition of a television personality. I was looking for guilt—I had to find out if you really were as innocent as you seemed.'

'That means you didn't think I was innocent that time you let me go. That time you came and handed me my car keys.'

'You have a tremendous amount to forgive me for,' he said gravely.

And when Darcy just smiled up at him, letting him know there was nothing she wouldn't forgive him, he

just had to kiss her, and kiss her again. And only when
he had at last drawn back did he say, emotion of that
kiss, the desire for her there in his eyes:

'I didn't want to let you go then. I'd kissed you, and
it did nothing to ease the wanting of you that had started
to grow in me. I knew before I let you go I was in love
with you. I wanted to keep you here with me, wanted
you to love me. But it was all new to me—this loving,
this torment of jealousy that devastated me every time I
thought of you with Stoddart—you with any man but
me. Oh, how I love you, Darcy!' he groaned. And to her
delight he gathered her tightly to him and smothered her
face with kisses.

When his mouth finally settled over hers, she felt
heady with that fire of yearning he had aroused in her
before. When his hands came to caress her breasts, she
was breathless with her need for him. For frantic
minutes they kissed and clung, his need for her un-
mistakable when at last they drew apart.

'Neve! Oh, Neve,' she breathed huskily, her face
flushed, desire for him in her eyes.

'Bear with me, my love,' he said, not looking apologetic at all for what he had created in her, a satisfaction in
him as he saw the way she was looking at him. 'I'm
thirty-seven, new to love. All I know for sure is that I
love you, am going to marry you, and that I have a lot
to make up for in that when I only ever wanted to be
nice to you, I always ended up being the exact opposite.'

Darcy sighed, her smile rejoicing. She had his love;
what else mattered? 'You were kind sometimes,' she
said, and gently teasing, 'And it wasn't all horrible,' and
was fascinated again as Neve grinned, as he too remembered those lovemaking moments.

'My sweet darling virgin,' he said, and Darcy knew
more joy as she coloured at his words, at his belief in
what she had at that first meeting told him. She didn't
know how she could take more joy, when observing the
pink in her face, he lovingly told her, 'With Emmy's

room being next to yours until you move into mine, I think we'd better see that preacher without delay, sweetheart,—don't you?'

Darcy could not think of one single objection to put to that idea—she couldn't wait!

THE GRIN OF THE CHESHIRE CAT

When someone "grins like a Cheshire cat," the way Blair does at Darcy in *Distrust Her Shadow*, it can be quite annoying—because such a grin has motives that are suspect. The Cheshire cat is one of the extraordinary creatures found in Lewis Carroll's book *Alice's Adventures in Wonderland*.

The story begins when a little girl named Alice follows a white rabbit down a hole. She finds herself in a most unusual place where she begins a series of strange adventures. She meets a menagerie of characters, such as the caterpillar who sits on a mushroom blowing smoke rings, the Mad Hatter who gives a wild tea party, the March Hare and the Queen of Hearts.

Wandering through the forest, Alice encounters a Cheshire cat, wearing a great gleeful smile and sitting in a tree. Alice is very surprised because she has never seen a cat smile before. They have a rather pleasant conversation, and the cat directs her to the Mad Hatter's tea party before vanishing abruptly into thin air! As Alice makes her way along, the cat reappears, and Alice tells it not to vanish so quickly. Still smiling, the cat disappears slowly, beginning with the end of its tail and working its way up until all that is left is the grin suspended in midair. "It's the most curious thing I ever saw in all my life!" declares Alice.

The encounter with the Cheshire cat is typical of the bizarre adventures Alice had. No wonder this delightful book has been translated into almost fifty languages, and gives such joy to children the world over!